B U R I E D

A **GOTH GIRL** MYSTERY

B U R I E D

linda joy singleton

Woodbury, Minnesota

First Edition
First Printing, 2012

Book design by Bob Gaul
Cover design by Kevin R. Brown
Cover art: Woman © iStockphoto.com/Don Bayley
      Heart © iStockphoto.com/elzeva
      Frame © iStockphoto.com/Katrin Solansky

Flux, an imprint of Llewellyn Worldwide Ltd.

Library of Congress Cataloging-in-Publication Data
Singleton, Linda Joy.
  Buried: a Goth girl mystery/Linda Joy Singleton.—1st ed.
    p. cm.
  Summary: Goth girl Thorn and her family move to Nevada where Thorn meets a mysterious masked guy and follows psychic vibrations from a locket to a shocking secret that has been buried for a long time.
  ISBN 978-0-7387-1958-0
[1. Psychic ability.—Fiction. 2. Supernatural.—Fiction. 3. Goth culture.—Fiction. 4. Nevada.—Fiction. 5. Mystery and detective stories.] I. Title.
PZ7.S6177Bu 2012
[Fic]—dc23

2011036325

Flux
Llewellyn Worldwide Ltd.
2143 Wooddale Drive
Woodbury, MN 55125-2989
www.fluxnow.com

Printed in the United States of America

Thank you to all the librarians and teachers who share their love of books with young readers. Your dedication and enthusiasm helped the Seer series reach many readers and spin off into new stories starring Goth Girl Thorn.

Special thanks to:

Maria Murillo
Kathy Spielman
Alma Prieto
Jennifer Rummel
Jennifer Collier
Diane Christensen
Sally McGrath

A seven-year-old girl was forced to marry a dog to ward off an evil curse," Rune announces as she pulls up a chair beside me on the semi-darkened stage in the school auditorium. She's all dark drama, with black eyeliner, blood-glossed lips, and pronounce-me-dead face makeup, and she thrives on saying shocking things.

Shocking works for me, so I scoot closer, my thrift-store army boots scraping the shiny wood floor.

"Have you ever heard anything so sick, Thorn?" she asks.

"Never!" I say with exaggerated disbelief, knowing that's what Rune expects and not wanting to disappoint. We haven't known each other long but were fated to be BFFs; not just because we're the only goths in our ultra-conservative school, but because she's the polar opposite of boring.

Every day she comes up with weird facts that sound unbelievable. Like yesterday, she told me about a woman who saved a chicken by giving it mouth-to-beak resuscitation. Rune has this theory that like the moon, the earth has

1

a light side and a dark side, but on earth the darkness comes from human beings. She insists her weird facts are evidence that modern civilization is deteriorating.

I can't speak for the rest of civilization, but after what I found this morning, I'm afraid things at my house are fast deteriorating. Only I don't want to think about this, so I gesture for Rune to go on.

"Girl Marries Dog," she announces as she unzips her backpack and withdraws her lunch—an apple and an energy drink. "That was today's headline on the *Weird News* site."

"You think that's bad?" I loosen the spiked collar that's been chafing my neck. "Catherine the Great of Russia was in love with her horse."

"But did they get married?"

"Don't think so."

"Well, I think forcing a little girl into an interspecies marriage is unnatural." Rune takes a bite of her apple and pauses to chew before adding, "Yet tragically true."

"You can't believe everything you read online."

"This site only reports authentic news. For the sake of that poor girl, I hope the dog was a family pet, not a stray. A stray would be filthy and have fleas."

"Better hygiene than the guys around here," I can't resist adding, since Rune and I are always complaining that we'll grow old as virgins because cool guys are a rare and mysterious species at Nevada Bluff High.

Rune nods. "The Cowboys are disgustingly proud of their spitting skills and sweat."

"I'd take sweat over gag-me cologne. Preps like the Jay-Clones are worst."

"Another tragically true fact," Rune says like she's telling a joke, but neither of us smile or (heaven forbid!) giggle. Giggling like cheerleaders is something we scorn, so we just share an understanding nod, not saying anything else while she pops open her energy drink.

I don't take my lunch out of my backpack because I'm not hungry.

Okay … that's not really the reason. I have to be honest with myself, if not anyone else. My reluctance to eat has nothing to do with appetite, and everything to do with avoidance. I glance uneasily at my backpack. I do *not* want to open it. Buried underneath books, assignments, and my sack lunch is the letter my mother never expected me to find.

A normal person wouldn't have found it, tucked under a Bible inside a drawer of Mom's desk. But before leaving for school this morning, I got one of my *feelings* and just knew it was there. And I knew from the first line—*the serious and very alarming matter of your eldest daughter*—that I was in trouble. Since then, my emotions have jumped from outrage to anxiety. Now I'm imploding inside and want to scream at someone, or maybe just talk.

I consider confiding in Rune.

Only I don't … because I'll have to either lie or reveal my three secrets.

Secret #1: First Names. I'm sure hers isn't Rune any more than mine is Thorn, but we have an unspoken understanding not to talk about it. So I don't ask and neither does she, which heightens our trust in each other. We're a lot alike—not just on the outside, draped in black and metal with wicked piercings, but deeper, like soul sisters. If I show her the letter, I know she'll be on my side and say things that will make me feel better.

But she might also say, "How did you find a letter that was inside your mom's desk?"

No. I'd better keep the letter—and my secrets—to myself.

"Where's Amerie? She's late." I glance at my rhinestone clock ring. The ring was a great find (only $2.95) at a secondhand shop called Hand-Me-Ups. At the time, I was only wearing eight rings and couldn't resist one more. Usually I enjoy hearing it tick when everything around me goes quiet, but now it's just another annoyance in an already bite-me bad day.

"Dunno what's up with Amerie." Rune's shrug swings her pink-streaked black braids over her mocha shoulders. "She was all acting mysterious when she said to meet here."

"But why here?" I gesture around the cavernous auditorium, which is not someplace Thorn and I usually hang out. Amerie, on the other hand, thrives on anything to do with theater. She also thrives on punctuality, usually.

"I bet it's about the Singing Star competition. Ever since Amerie volunteered to help with it, she's been totally obsessed." Rune rolls her kohl-shadowed eyes. "Can you believe she asked me to sign up, even though I can't sing?"

"Your voice doesn't suck but contests do."

"I told her I'd only do it if I could sing about weird facts."

"Like the dog wedding," I say, grinning.

"I'll bring my dog and hum a wedding tune."

"As your bridesmaid, I'll throw doggie treats instead of flowers."

"Yum," she jokes, pantomiming begging like a dog.

"You really are a sick puppy."

"And proud of it." Rune tilts her dark head and flashes me a challenging grin. "Gonna sign up?"

"Don't be insane," I say, sharper than I intend.

"You play a mean guitar and your voice isn't bad either."

"Messing around my guitar is just for fun. And karaoke is not singing. You swore never to mention my unfortunate lapse in judgment."

"I'd never tell anyone else, but can't we talk about it? We're alone in here, so no one else can hear. But people should hear you sing and play guitar. You're, like, multi-talented. If you entered, you could win."

"Win what? Public humiliation?" I pick up a napkin from our makeshift lunch table and flick it at her. "No way."

She catches it and wipes her hands. "Seriously, Thorn, you should do this."

"Subject dropped." I shake my head like this is the dumbest thing she's ever said, but she's struck a nerve.

Secret #2: Dreams of Being a Professional Musician. Music matters more to me than I care to admit. It's like if I speak this dream, it'll shatter and die. Still, sometimes I allow myself to imagine strumming a guitar and performing my own songs in off-the-path cafés. My blood is infused with rhythm and I only feel whole when I'm lost in a song.

Lately I've even been thinking that maybe … just maybe … I might be good. But I'd never enter a talent show, especially at school, so I say in my firmest tone, "I don't believe in contests."

"Why not?" Rune's pierced brows rise.

"They're exploitive and unfairly judge people based on biased and subjective opinions. I absolutely refuse to enter. If that's why Amerie asked us to meet us here, I'm gonna be pissed."

Checking my clock-ring again, I scowl.

Talking about singing and not talking about the letter has me on edge, but there's something else, too. Ever since I walked into this hushed, empty auditorium, I've had a creepy feeling. Like some invisible something is watching. And I can't shake it off, even though it's obvious Rune and I are the only ones here.

I order myself to stop stressing and pull my lunch bag from my backpack (carefully avoiding the letter) and eat my sandwich, chips, and carrot sticks. Lunch is like the only "exhale" part of the school schedule, when I can hang out with my best friends and talk about interesting stuff like tat art, vampirism, music, and theories about how the education system conspires to turn kids into obedient robots. The whole grade system is bogus, forcing unique personalities into A, B, C, D, and F categories. I choose E—*none of the above*. Why does any one person have to excel in all subjects? If we were all the same, we'd come in Barbie-sized boxes and have Mattel stamped on our plastic butts.

Fortunately, not all school is brain numbing. I've just

come from my lit class where Ms. Chu read from a verse novel about dead mothers. Lit is my only nontorturous class. The rest are so boring, I find myself staring out the window and mouthing words to songs that only I can hear.

I'm startled to actually hear music. But it's very real and coming from Rune's earphones. Rune leans back in her chair; her eyes are closed as she taps her purple-tipped, two-inch-long fingernails to death rock.

She doesn't notice when I turn away, my hand trailing along the metal curve of my chair as my thoughts drift with my gaze. It's weird being on the stage, with its deep blue velvet curtains sweeping off to the sides like wings ready to fly at the sound of applause. Not that I care about applause or acting or anything like that. The closest I've come is helping Amerie run her lines. Where is she, anyway?

Frustrated, I cross the stage and snoop in boxes stacked in a corner. I peek inside one labeled *Accessories* and find bizarre objects like false teeth with fangs, sequined high heels, a plastic bloody severed hand, and a scraggly black beard woven with plastic spiders. There are also random props against a back wall: a couch with mismatched cushions, a stuffed parrot in a cage, a wooden cane with a tiger's head, and a sarcophagus.

How would it feel to lie inside the sarcophagus? I think of the insanity level of my life with five siblings—it would be cool to have my own Egyptian-coffin retreat. Whenever I needed alone time, I'd climb inside and shut out the world until there was only silence. Except it would be cramped and stuffy and I might get claustrophobic.

Sucking in a deep breath, I turn back toward Rune. I take a few steps, then stop when I notice a circle of metal chairs, most facing in but several tilted at odd angles like a meeting had ended abruptly.

Golden light glints from one of the chairs.

A compelling feeling steals over me. Rushing wind roars in my head, making everything spin. Whirling, I'm losing myself. Something else is taking over.

Psychedelic colors explode around me as if I'm the nucleus of a wild storm. I struggle for control, but it's like being strapped in on a dizzying roller-coaster ride. I'm powerless and know there's no course except to surrender, because this has happened before—although never with such intensity.

I ride a wave of urgency, moving forward, stretching out my arm, reaching for an unknown something I must possess. My fingers curl around a necklace. A heart-shaped golden pendant the size of a quarter hangs on a black shoelace. It's shiny and tacky. Yet I can't resist clasping the pendant to my chest with a reverent, loving touch.

My touch changes everything.

I'm aware of being at school, yet I'm somewhere else, too—a night world where chilly wind bites my skin and sets me shivering. It's like being trapped inside a dream. Terrifying darkness surrounds me and I smell wild grasses and damp dirt. The only lights are far above, twinkling stars filtered by ominous clouds. Unseen forest creatures rustle around me, whispering in a conspiracy with shadowy trees. And a shrill cry like a dying animal pierces the night.

Not real, I tell myself. I'm not in the woods and it isn't night. There are no wild animals. I'm in the school auditorium in the middle of the day and none of this is happening.

As if my words summon power, I really am back at school.

I blink fast, confused and breathing heavily as if I've just run around the two-mile school track. I look down at my hand and see the necklace. I don't want it, but know it wants me. I glance over at Rune, who's still swaying with her headphones. She hasn't noticed anything.

Only seconds have passed, in a prophetic eclipse that only I could see.

Yet I'm not afraid. I've always had this freakish talent, and each experience is different. Sometimes I choose to touch the objects, and other times, like now, they choose me.

Secret #3: Psychometry.

I'm a Finder.

TWO

A slammed door shudders like thunder through the auditorium, and I hastily slip the necklace into my pocket.

Amerie skips down the aisle, glittery pink wings fluttering behind her. Yes, wings. Weird but true fact: lithe and petite Amerie would seem naked without her wings. She's into faeries and all things fantastical, and today she's wearing dance slippers and a loose cotton tunic over pink tights. She's so anti-goth, you'd think Rune and I would want nothing to do with her. But anyone who wears wings to school deserves props for bravery.

"Are you dying and totally miserable to find out my news?" Amerie exclaims as she pulls up a chair beside Rune. She tucks in her lacy wings so that only the glittery tips show behind her short, frizzy, light brown curls.

"Oh?" I say in this uber-bored tone as I sit down. Amerie means well but is prone to exaggeration. "You have news?"

"I never would have guessed," Rune adds as she slips off her headphones.

"Liars! It's obvious you're both ill with curiosity. And you should be, because what I have to tell you is going to blow your minds. I can't believe no one ever told me, or maybe they just didn't know. Who could have guessed this could happen at this nowhere-nothing school? And don't bother trying to guess, it's too incredible."

Rune turns to me with a long-suffering sigh. "She's babbling again, Thorn. Any idea why?"

"No clue." I shrug.

"Sounds like a serious malady that may need medical attention." Rune shakes her head gravely. "Babbling is an early sign of acute delusion."

"We could stage an intervention," I suggest. "I'll bring the straitjacket."

"Oh, stop." Amerie pinches fairy dust (glitter) off her wings and flicks it at me. "I should leave right now and not tell you anything, but you'll find out anyway because it's all over school. I mean, someone like that coming here is the hugest news in the universe. I'm still jazzed. He's going to be a judge and I'm on the audition committee."

As I shake the glittery dust from my wig, Rune and I exchange glances. You'd think we'd be used to Amerie's flights into fantasyland, but she doesn't make it easy. She's cool most of the time, but other times I just want to slap duct tape over her mouth.

"Is this about the singing contest?" I guess.

"Duh. Haven't you heard anything I said?" Amerie purses her glossy-peach lips. "If you'd just listen—"

"We're trying," Rune insists. "But you're not making any sense."

"Okay…I'll…go…slooooow. One word: Philippe."

"Philippe?" I repeat, sure I've heard wrong. "Not *the* *Philippe*?"

It's embarrasing to admit, but when Amerie nods, my mouth falls open. I usually mock the chronically music-impaired who listen to pop rock, but I'd have to be living in an alternate universe not to recognize the name. *Philippe.* Tall, bronzed, smoldering, with intense blue eyes and a wry charismatic smile. But what everyone really notices is his long, spiraling black hair. I heard his barber sold his hair cuttings on eBay for over five hundred dollars.

When I look at Rune, her mouth is open, too.

"At last I have your attention." Amerie smirks. "Philippe isn't his real name. He changed it and never talks about living here. But I checked my brother's yearbook from two years ago, and he's in there. Page thirty-two."

"Philippe went to our school?" I say incredulously.

"Shocking, huh?" Amerie nods. "Of course he looked way different, with wild dreds and baggy clothes. But I'd know his smile anywhere."

"Undeniably hot smile," Rune agrees. "Still, I can hardly believe a celebrity came from our hick school."

"When he went here, his name was Phil Wilkinson and he was a bad-ass, always getting into fights and expelled. Then he dropped out."

"And signed on with Montage Records." I remember seeing him on E-TV (not what I'd choose to watch, but I'm outvoted by my sibs) and crediting his stardom to being a Good Samaritan. He was discovered after helping a woman stranded on the road with a flat tire; she turned out to be the girlfriend of the cousin of a big-shot at Montage. Phil must have reformed from being a bad-ass or, more likely, the stranded woman was really hot and he'd hoped to hit on her.

"It's a real success story," Amerie says with a blissful sigh. "I'm thrilled Philippe is going to judge the Singing Star competition."

"Wow!" Rune shakes her head in awe. "Have you met him?"

"Why do you think I'm late? Today has been amazing crazy."

"You mean he's here?" Rune jumps up from her chair. "Today?"

"Right here, on this stage this morning." Amerie gestures to the chairs grouped together center-stage. "I'd heard we were going to have a guest judge, but had no idea who until he showed up during registration and offered to sign autographs and answer questions."

"And you didn't text me?" Rune gripes. "What kind of friend are you?"

"How could I? It was a mob scene. Besides, I knew you wouldn't take me seriously. You never do."

"You usually don't have anything interesting to share— not like my weird facts. You missed the one today about this girl marrying a dog."

While Rune fills Amerie in on the canine nuptials, I think fast, the stud in my tongue playing on my teeth. I stare at the chair where I found the necklace. The golden heart warms my pocket, but I resist the urge to touch it again. I don't want to freak out in front of my friends. I wonder who lost the necklace and why it triggered my radar. Not that anyone here knows what I can do. I mean, I don't want kids bugging me to find every little lost item or acting like I'm something special. Revealing my finding skill would be a no-win situation.

Still, I can't get the nightmare vision out of my head, so I ask Amerie if she remembers who was on stage with Philippe.

Amerie turns away from Rune. "I don't know exactly. Most of the girls in drama and even some guys. I was busy signing up talent. Speaking of which ... " She looks at us both pointedly.

"NO!" Rune and I both say before she can ask. I tell her firmly I don't do contests. And Rune chimes in with her claim of "no talent."

"It's your loss," Amerie says. "Only contestants get to meet Philippe."

Disappointment flickers on Rune's face, but she quickly hides it by picking up her backpack and slipping the strap over her shoulder. "I never download his sappy songs anyway. We better go, Thorn—I want to stop by my locker before next class."

"Yeah ... but wait." I'm compelled to reach into my pocket. I wind my fingers through the shoestring cord and slowly pull out the golden heart.

"What's that?" Rune asks.

"Something I just found. Amerie, do you recognize it?"

"No, and I usually notice jewelry, even poor-quality pieces like that."

"This isn't real gold?" I trust Amerie's opinion when it comes to jewelry because she really knows her stuff. She crafts her own line of silver and rock jewelry, selling it online and at Renaissance fairs.

"Definitely not gold—shiny yellow paint." She rubs her finger across the necklace. "Cheap metal, too, and hanging it on a shoelace instead of a chain is tacky."

"I found it on that chair over there. Any idea who was sitting there, Amerie?"

"As if I could remember? It was way too hectic and I hardly knew where *I* was, much less anyone else." Glitter sparkles in the air as Amerie shakes her head. "I mean, I was talking to everyone about the competition and explaining the sign-up procedures, when suddenly the door bursts open and Philippe, his manager, and a hulking guy who is obviously his bodyguard come in. Even my drama teacher begged for an autograph, and I nearly got trampled in the rush. Fortunately Philippe's manager made everyone sit down so he could answer questions."

"Isn't there any way of finding out who owns this?" I hold out my hand again; the gold-painted necklace looks plain and insignificant in my open palm. For a second I feel dizzy and smell the damp earth. I sense emotions, too; an overwhelming sadness, as if tragedy is connected to this necklace.

Amerie gives me a curious look. "Why do you care anyway?"

"Who said I cared?" I shrug. "Just curious who lost this."

Rune snorts. "That necklace is butt ugly. It wasn't lost—it was abandoned."

"Even tacky jewelry has sentimental value to someone," Amerie says. "Leave it with me, Thorn, and I'll ask around. If no one claims it, I'll drop it off at the Lost and Found."

This sounds sensible and I'm grateful to Amerie. But when I reach to hand the necklace over to her, my fingers cramp up and won't release. I try to open my hand, but I just can't do it.

"Uh...maybe I better keep it for now." I slip my hand into my jeans pocket, where my fingers loosen and the necklace slips out easily.

"You sure?" Amerie asks.

"You've got enough going on. You don't need added stress."

The necklace wants me but I don't want it.

Finding is just something I can do; it's not a real skill like music or singing. Sure, it's come in handy a few times—once I even helped save someone from suicide—but being able to find things isn't magic. It's just a freaky trait, like wiggling your ears or touching your nose with your tongue.

During my next class, Spanish, I put the necklace in a zipper pocket of my backpack. I force myself to concentrate while Señor Rojas hammers Spanish phrases into our heads. My gaze shifts to my backpack just as Señor Rojas asks me something in Spanish.

Huh? My mind blanks and I stare at him, aware that the rest of the class is staring at me. Underneath my powder-pale makeup, I know my cheeks are burning.

"Por favor, repita la pregunta," I say.

"Conteste a la pregunta, por favor," Señor Rojas responds, not giving me a break.

"¿Um ... quién posee el collar?"

Where did that come from? I wonder, having no idea what I just said.

I touch the spiked collar around my neck, knowing by the laughter spilling around me that I've said something dumb. I want to ask the teacher what I said, but Señor Rojas just shakes his head at me like I'm a hopeless waste of time. Then he turns to another student.

It's not until I'm leaving fifth period that I remember what *collar* means in Spanish: necklace.

My last class, U.S. History, is my best and worst. Best because when it's over, so is school. Worst because my teacher, Mr. Sproat, hates me. Nothing new really, since most adults are suspicious of teens wearing corpse makeup, black clothes, and metal spikes. But Mr. Sproat doesn't scorn in silence, and since witch burnings haven't been legal in this country since the 1700s, he's found another way to torture me. On my first day in his class, he called me to the front of the room and asked loudly, "Isn't it a little early to be costumed for Halloween?" I would have rather been burned at the stake. Ironically, Mr. Sproat is also an excellent teacher, bringing history alive with the skill of a born storyteller. I'd really like U.S. History if he weren't such an asshole.

So I keep my head low and avoid all conflict. But when I hear a shrill cry like a child or animal in pain, I slap my hand over my mouth so I won't gasp. When no one else seems to notice anything odd, I'm afraid I'm going crazy—especially since the sound came from my backpack.

That damn necklace.

Stealthily, I reach into my backpack. There's another cry, like the necklace is calling to me, and I can't resist lifting it, the golden heart warm against my palms. I'm overwhelmed with a desire to caress the glossy surface and slip the shoelace around my neck. But I don't want to wear it—*it wants to wear me.*

Delusional, I tell myself. *Got to get out of here. Now.*

So I suck up my courage and raise my hand. I ask Mr. Sproat if I can go to the restroom. He taps his fingers on his desk and fixes me with a narrow stare. "If you're not back in ten minutes," he warns, "there will be dire consequences."

I grab my backpack when Mrs. Sproat's back is turned, then go before he changes his mind.

Once outside, inhaling deep breaths of crisp October air, I feel better. I don't actually need a restroom but head for one anyway. My boots clomp-echo on the walkway, reminding me that I'm a square peg in this round world of gleaming windows and ultra-modern architecture. Nevada Bluff High, with its connecting rows of classrooms and open-air design, is more like an outdoor mall than a school. Everything has a western theme; bucking broncos are carved on columns, a rodeo mural trails across the outside wall of the administration building, and there's a fountain shaped like a horseshoe.

The unofficial uniform here is denim, cotton, and western hats. Even for the teachers.

My last school, Sheridan High in California, wasn't much to look at—boxy classrooms in need of new paint and out-of-date equipment—but there were lovely shade trees and emerald-green lawns. After living in Nevada these past few months, I'm longing for the color green. In the high desert it's more common to see tumbleweeds cartwheeling across a patch of rocky weeds than grass or shade trees. Yards are creatively landscaped with cactus, driftwood, and rocks. Hardly anyone has lawn; it's like it's outlawed.

Sometimes I feel outlawed too. My father still scowls when I leave for school in my wigs, piercings, and death-black clothes. When I first started NB High, kids pointed and snickered at me. I ignored them because, frankly, I don't give a crap what they think. Why should I? Judgmental lemmings aren't worth my brain-space. It's funny, though, because the more I don't care, the less they point. Some even wave.

A strange feeling creeps over me and I walk right past the restroom. I don't understand the compulsion that forces me to lift my gaze beyond the classrooms to the dark silhouette on the hill. The old gym. The decaying building is off-limits, dangerous, and completely forbidden to students.

As a rule, I don't follow rules.

"Field trip," I murmur, grinning as I step off the cement walkway.

What did Amerie tell me about the old gym? It's all that's left from the original high school, which was demolished after a generous donation from Judge Blankenship funded the new high school. Oh yeah—the old gym is supposed to be haunted. Ha! Rune clued me in on this scare-tactic rumor. But even if the gym *is* haunted (which I doubt), I've seen ghosts before and they don't scare me.

Well ... not much.

Hiking up the hill is harder than it looks; the steep terrain is rough with rocks and scratchy bushes. Students back in the old-gym days must have been part mountain goat. Brittle weeds crackle under my feet as I near the crumbling foundation of the old building. A brisk wind slithers through my shirt and I tuck my hands into my jeans pocket for warmth. When my fingertips touch the necklace an eerie feeling steals over me. I take deep breaths to clear my head.

What's going on? I study the necklace. It's cheap and ordinary yet it's freaking me out. I don't need this stress. My life has more than enough already since moving here (thank you very much, Mom!). For the first time ever, my two brothers and three sisters and I united in protest. None of us wanted to move. But it was useless. Dad's unemployment checks were running out, so when Mom got the offer to be the minister of a small church in Nevada Bluff—a job that came with a large farmhouse, rent-free—she accepted without even holding a family meeting.

Sucks, but I've adjusted. Still, the last thing I need is a tacky necklace messing with my head.

Up close, the old gym looks less mysterious and more old and pathetic. When I glance at my clock-ring, I debate whether or not to go back to class. Twelve of my ten minutes are up. Trouble is no longer an option but a foregone conclusion.

There's nothing exciting here, so I start back. But I only take a few steps before something clangs, like metal smashing against a wall. Then a blood-curdling cry comes from inside the gym.

At first I think the gym really is haunted—until I hear a very human voice shout "Help!"

Gritting my teeth, I think of all the times I've been sucked into other people's problems. I don't want to get involved. But when a thundering crash echoes so loudly I nearly jump out of my army boots, I stare at the gym: its busted windows, sagging timbers, and peeling paint. My heart races as I imagine someone trapped inside.

How can I just walk away?

I creep up to a rusted door that's hanging off its hinges. Leaning forward, I peer into gloomy darkness. Light streams down through holes in the ceiling, but I can't see more than vague shapes of old furniture and what might have once been bathroom stalls.

I hear "Help!" again and squeeze through the half-open door. Dust stirs under my shoes and my nose itches like I'm going to sneeze. The air stinks with decay and foul smells that make me think of dead things.

Up ahead, a wall of silver gleams. Not a wall, I realize as I walk toward it, but a towering steel cage for gym equipment. Only instead of sports equipment, there's a guy locked inside!

Before I can help, I sense movement from a side corridor:

a tall shadowy figure swathed in black jeans, boots, a long dark coat, and a black knit ski mask with eye slits. He looks so surreal that at first I think he's a ghost who will float through me. But he radiates a powerful confidence that's totally human.

He swivels, slowly, his piercing black eyes fixed on me like a hunter sighting his rifle on his prey.

I would have preferred a ghost.

THREE

I spin around and run like crazy across the dusty floor, back through the half-hinged door and outside. Gulping fresh air, I don't stop to look behind me when I hear a shout and pounding footsteps. If I can just get down the hill and back to school, then I'll be safe and can get help for the kid trapped inside the equipment cage.

The footsteps come closer. I hear my pursuer's heavy breaths.

Hurry, hurry! I urge myself.

I'm nearly to the downhill stretch of smoother terrain when I stumble over a rock. My feet fly out from beneath me. I'm falling, falling—until a strong gloved hand grabs my arm. Jerked around, I face hostile black eyes.

"Who the hell are you?" Masked Guy demands in a deep but young voice. It sounds like he's my age.

"Who's asking?" I try to break free but his grip is steel.

"If you haven't figured it out yet, you will soon. You're

one of those goths—the new girl." It wasn't a question; more of an accusation. "What are you doing here?"

Despite the sweat trickling down my back, I keep my voice calm like I'm lacking the fear gene. "I'd ask you that question, except I don't care enough."

"You're off-campus in a restricted area. Why?" A gust of wind flaps his coat, but he doesn't loosen his grip on my arm. "Were you spying on me?"

"Paranoid much?" I shake my head. "I don't even know who you are."

"You don't?" His tone is edged in suspicion like he's calling me a liar.

"Don't know and don't care."

"Didn't you notice the 'condemned' signs?" He gestures toward signs on the sagging remains of a fence. "Even a new student should know this area is off-limits and extremely dangerous."

"You're here. And so is that poor guy you locked in there." I point to the old gym. "You'd better let him out."

"Don't worry about him." Masked Guy releases my hand and pushes me away. "Go back to class before you get in trouble."

I'm bristling inside, tempted to reach out and rip off his black mask.

"Go on. Get out of here," he orders.

"I'm not leaving until you let that guy out of the cage." I glare him down like we're in a competition of wills.

His black eyes glare even fiercer. "You have no idea

who you're messing with. I have urgent things to do. Leave now or—"

"Or what? Are you going to do to me whatever you did to that kid in there?" I plant my hands on my hips, challenging him. Sure, he's taller and stronger, but if he was a real threat he'd have done something already. I'm starting to think he's just a student breaking rules. Like me.

Besides, I may not look strong, but I can defend myself. I glance down at the third finger on my right hand. The gold and metal ring there is more than a wicked accessory—with a flick of my touch, the prong will stick up into a sharp sword-like spike. A gift from my honorary brother, K.C., who survived living on the streets until my family took him in. People underestimated him, too.

Masked Guy shakes his head. "That guy isn't going to be hurt—but I can't promise what'll happen if you don't get out of here. I don't have time for this."

"I got loads of time." I glance at my clock-ring. I've been gone for over twenty minutes. Between Mr. Sproat, the freaky necklace, and worrying about the letter hidden in my backpack, I'm already buried in trouble without a shovel to dig myself out. A little more won't matter. I refuse to back down to this jerk.

"Nice mask," I say with thick sarcasm. "Did your grandma knit it for you?"

"Gran doesn't knit—she's too busy kickboxing."

"Does she fight your battles for you when you're not hiding under a mask?"

I expect him to get mad, but he chuckles. "Most girls

would be scared and run away. But you're different. I don't know if that's a good thing or bad."

"Bad news for you if you don't let that guy go." I gesture toward the gym. "You could get arrested for kidnapping."

"So call the cops—just do it somewhere else."

"If you won't let him out, then I will!"

I lunge forward but he's faster, an impassible wall blocking my way back to the gym. "Don't even try. Turn around and go back to school like a smart girl."

Being threatened is bad enough, but being patronized is worse. Now I'm really pissed off.

"Who is the guy you've got in there?" I demand, lifting my chin to meet his narrow-slit gaze.

"Someone who deserves worse than I'm giving him. If you knew what he did, you'd lock him in a cage too."

"I seriously doubt that." I kick at a weed that's snagged a shoelace hanging from my boot. "Is this some dumb initiation into a Masked Geek Club, or is that guy hurt? What did you do to him?"

"Me?" He points to himself with a fake innocent tone, and I'm sure he's grinning underneath his black mask. "Don't you know that making such a serious accusation is slanderous? I could sue you and financially ruin your family."

I almost laugh. "If my family had anything worth suing for, I wouldn't be stuck living in this brain-numbing hellhole."

"Not a fan of Nevada Bluff High?"

"Not a fan of Nevada."

"Those are fighting words at a school where school pride

runs high. Haven't you heard NB is number one in the high school football league and the alma mater of the last five county rodeo champions?"

The dry irony in his tone makes it impossible to tell if he's poking fun at the school or at me. "I don't give a crap about this school or you. I wouldn't bother with that guy if I knew he'd be okay. I have enough troubles already." I glance uneasily at my backpack.

In the distance, a bell announces the end of the school day.

Masked Guy lifts his head so I know he heard the bell, too, and he tenses as if growing anxious. "This ends now," he says roughly. "You're leaving."

"Sure." I smile like I'm sweet and gullible.

"Then get moving."

"Whatever you say." I take a step toward the gym.

"Not in there!" he shouts.

"Putting someone's life in danger is just stupid and dangerous." I race toward the gym door but before I can make it, Masked Guy's gloved hand springs out. He grabs my arm and spins me around, pinning me against his chest.

"Let me go!" I squirm, kicking his leg and feeling some satisfaction when I hear him grunt in pain.

"I've played nice until now," he growls. "No more."

"Are you threatening me?"

"I never threaten." He's close enough for me to feel his hot breath on my neck and catch a whiff of musky cologne. "I act," he says.

Then he yanks my backpack from my shoulder and

shoves me roughly to the ground. "You'll find this in the Dumpster by the library," he says. "But you'd better hurry because someone else may find it first—and you know how dishonest students can be in this hellhole."

Then he strides off with my backpack.

I stumble to my feet, shaking with fury, and see the back of his head—and the bright yellow design on his ski mask.

A cheerful smiley face.

Mocking me.

FOUR

ive me my backpack!" I shout, but my words drift away
like dead leaves in the wind.

I look at the gym, wanting to rescue the kid trapped
inside, but I'm sure his cage is locked and I'd end up going
for help anyway.

So I take off down the rough terrain after the Masked
Guy. He's moving fast, like he's part goat and part track star.
I shout after him again but he's so far away that all I can
make out is a dark blur. My army boot smacks a boulder and
I stumble, somersaulting onto prickly weeds. My jeans rip
and my knees sting, but my pride hurts worse.

Panic grows because I can *not* lose my backpack. Not
only does it have expensive-to-replace school books, but I'd
die if anyone—especially a masked jerk—read the letter.
There's the heart-shaped necklace, too, which I don't want to
keep but ache at the thought of losing.

So I run like I'm in a life-or-death race. The terrain rises,
then drops at a steep angle. I veer around a large rock, then

peer down the hill at the school; it seems as small as a string of toy blocks linked together. I don't see Masked Guy.

He's probably already at the Dumpster, I think with a new burst of anger. My lungs ache as I leave the rocky dirt and sprint on the smooth school pavement.

Kids cram the walkways after the final bell, and I weave through the crowds murmuring "sorry" whenever I bump someone. What Dumpster did he say? Oh, yeah, the library. Only I'm going the wrong direction, so I turn around and take a sharp right down a narrow path. The *Library* plaque flashes by and I keep going until I reach the Dumpster.

I reach out and lift up the lid, holding my breath as I stand on my toes to peer inside. Yes! Exhaling, I rescue my backpack.

Immediately, I check inside and am relieved that nothing is missing. Wallet, keys, gold necklace, and the letter I found in Mom's desk. I sling my backpack over my shoulder then turn around and head for Ms. Chu's classroom. She's the only teacher who will believe me when I tell her a masked guy kidnapped someone—probably a student from our school—and locked him in a cage.

But as I pass the quad, which offers a view back up the hill, I see several distant figures hurrying toward the old gym. At least one person is an adult, probably a teacher or the principal. Help is on the way for the trapped guy, which is a huge relief. He'll be rescued—and I won't have to deal with telling Ms. Chu a bizarre story.

After a quick stop at my locker, I walk past buses spewing

diesel fumes and cars jam-packed on the street to meet Rune at our usual place by the school flagpole.

Rune takes one look at me and points. "Why is there a banana peel on your backpack? Are bananas the latest in goth fashion?"

"Not funny." Angry all over again, I yank off my backpack to grab the strip of banana peel. Then I stomp over to a nearby trash can and toss the offending bits of brown and yellow away.

"Were you attacked by a banana-flinging monkey?" When I glare at her, she grins. "Did you know that in Alabama there's a grave where people leave bananas instead of flowers? It's for a space monkey that returned alive. But now she's dead and all those bananas just rot on the grave."

"Rune, I've had a crappy day and if you want to survive long enough to hear about it, you will shut up right now. Let's just go somewhere to talk."

"Okay—what's going on?" She frowns at my dusty, ripped jeans. "Did you get run over by a truck or something?"

"Or something," I say wearily.

Instead of walking home (a mile to her house together, then a mile to mine alone), Rune leads me to our favorite hangout, The Hole Truth donut shop.

"SOS! Donut crisis," Rune calls out as we enter the shop. The Hole Truth doubles as a thrift store, its shelves full of glass figurines, bobble heads, and holiday decorations. The linoleum floor is faded and the ceiling leaks during rain. But it's a haven for us, and the owner, a half-Mexican/ half-African American elderly man named Antonio, always knows exactly what his customers need, prescribing the right donut like a doctor prescribes pain-killers.

Antonio takes one look at me and shakes his balding dark head, then leads us to our usual booth in the back underneath a shelf of Halloween decorations. "Rough day?" he asks me sympathetically.

"Apocalyptic." I nod, sitting across from Rune on a cracked leather seat.

"She'll need a double dose," Rune says grimly. She reaches for the napkin container and peels off a napkin for me.

I murmur "thanks" and wipe banana mush from my hands.

"I have the perfect remedy," Antonio says in a rolling Spanish accent. "You sit here and I'll bring it out pronto."

When he's gone, Rune takes off her studded leather jacket and flips her braids back. "Tell me everything."

I bite my lip, not sure where to start and wishing I could just forget about it.

"Come on, Thorn, let go of negativity. Don't hold it inside and pollute your psyche." Rune is hardcore into alternative thinking and holds unique views on life, connected to nature. I've learned a lot from her. But I'm reluctant to admit a masked guy made a fool of me.

I get a temporary reprieve when Antonio sweeps toward us balancing a vintage Care Bear metal TV tray on one hand. He slides the tray onto the table with a dramatic flourish.

"Antonio's pastry prescription to vanish the bad-day blues," the old man says with a pearly white grin. "Take two glazed cake donuts filled with whipped cream and sprinkled with caramel. Enjoy!"

Donuts soothe better than mind-numbing drugs, and when I'm finished licking whipped cream off my lips, I'm finally ready to talk.

So I tell Rune everything: the hike to the old gym, the guy trapped in a cage, masked dude stealing my backpack, and the group of rescuers headed to the gym. When I finish, Rune stares at me, her mouth hanging open with utter shock.

"I should have gone back to help the trapped guy," I add guiltily. "But I'm sure he's okay now. I handled everything really stupidly. Don't hate me."

"OMG! I don't hate you—I want to be you!" she exclaims, her kohl-shaded eyes almost popping out. "Do you have any idea who you just met?"

"I have no idea who was in the cage."

"Not him! The masked dude."

I stare at her like she's deranged and wonder if it's possible for someone to get high on donuts.

"You really don't know?" Rune asks incredulously.

"Know what? That my best friend is loco? Yes, I do know that. But I never realized it was this bad."

"Thorn, seriously, you don't get it." She's practically jumping in her chair. "That masked guy is legend! I'm shocked you don't know. Everyone at school does."

"He was wearing a mask. How was I supposed to know?"

"Of course he wears a mask. That's how he got his nickname."

"Huh?" I blink, confused.

"Everyone calls him the Grin Reaper."

"Isn't that the mythological devil dude who foretells deaths?"

"Not the *Grim* Reaper—the *Grin* Reaper because of the smiley face on his mask and the smiley face stickers he leaves with his victims."

Now I know my best friend has completely lost it. "You're punking me, right?"

"He's for real, and last year the whole school was buzzing about him. He only goes after students who deserve it. The Grin Reaper is like the best bad dude ever."

"You admire him? Even after he attacked me and threw me on the ground?"

Rune frowns. "He isn't usually violent."

"Well, he was with me. I can't believe you're defending him."

"If you'd gone here last year, you would too," she tells me. "Everyone is sure he's a student here but no one has a clue who he really is." She looks down at the table, her purple-tipped fingers twining together. "He's the only non-boring guy at school. Ever since I heard about him, I've thought... well... it would be cool to see him."

"You've never seen him?"

"No one has—except his victims."

"That would include me." I hold out my wrists, which are red and starting to bruise.

She purses her black-shimmered lips and pauses as if thinking deeply before lowering her voice to a whisper. "I doubt he meant to hurt you. You were just in his way. The guy in his cage was his target. The Grin Reaper is all about getting justice."

"Justice?" I laugh bitterly. "You can't be serious! That dude is dangerous."

"Dangerous is my flavor of hot." Rune sighs in this dreamy way which is so not like her. "We'd be great together—but his identity is a huge mystery. Sometimes I dream we're alone together and he's taking off his mask just for me. I'm excited that I'm finally going to see his face. Only I wake up. I'd give anything to know what's under that mask."

"An arrogant, domineering, egotistical jerk," I rant. "He locked a guy in a decaying gym, attacked me, then threw my backpack in a Dumpster."

"I'm sure he had a good reason."

I toss my crumpled napkin at her. "Is there ever a good reason for kidnapping and violence?"

"He's not like that," she says defensively. "The Grin Reaper only goes after people who deserve to be punished. Last year, a senior named Clem shaved the fur off a stray dog that hung around school. When Principal Niphai found out, instead of punishing Clem he called the pound on the dog. Next day, Clem was attacked by a guy in a smiley face ski mask and two words were written in indelible ink on his forehead: *Dog Abuser*."

"So?" I raise my brows.

"That was the first time. A month later, a soccer coach kicked a kid off the team because he'd come out as gay. Next day, there were Photoshopped pictures all over school of the coach wearing only a pink bra and lace panties. On the back of each photo was a smiley face sticker. After that the smiley faced vigilante became known as the 'Grin Reaper.'"

"Okay, so maybe those guys deserved it, but that doesn't make up for what the masked guy did to me. You wouldn't make excuses for him if you'd been there."

"I wish I had been," Rune says wistfully. "Except for his victims, you're only person who's actually heard his voice."

"Lucky me," I say sarcastically. I've never seen Rune so brain-scrambled over a guy and frankly, it's disturbing. "Snap out of your twisted hero worship and accept that the guy is a menace. I may be okay, but I have no idea how the caged guy is doing."

"I can find out." Rune fishes her phone from a pocket in her oversized black-sequined sweater. "News spreads fast, so half the school will know by now."

I watch over her shoulder as she texts Amerie. I should have thought of calling Amerie. Our fairy-winged friend devours gossip blogs and knows everything practically before it happens.

"Good news, Thorn," Rune says a short while later, after her phone beeps with a new text. "The caged guy is fine."

My guilt eases. "I'm glad that poor kid is okay."

"That 'poor kid' is Brute—I mean, Bruce—Gibson," Rune tells me as she pays the check and we leave the donut shop. "He's built like a wrestler and a loyal Jay-Clone—our favorite subhuman group."

I cringe at the mention of the preppy crowd that sucks up to Jay Blankenship because his father is Judge Blankenship, whose wallet funds school programs. The five guys strut around in fancy blue letter jackets—not for real sports like basketball or football, but for golf. Spoiled rich brats who think they own the school.

"This morning, Brute pranked a freshman from the Special Ed class," Rune continues as we wait on the curb for traffic to pass. Her gaze is half on the road and half on her phone. She texts *Thx* back to Amerie, then slips her phone in her pocket. "Shoved the freshman into a locker and left him there for over an hour. Brute got off as usual, since he denied it and his Jay-Clone pals backed him up."

"They're the worst," I agree.

"The Grin Reaper's justice was perfect." Rune grins. "I'm glad he's back in action. I thought maybe he'd graduated or dropped out since he hadn't struck this year—but now I think he must still be a student here. I'd give anything to meet him."

"Don't talk stupid."

"So he's a little unorthodox in his methods."

"He attacked me." I lift my bruised wrists to remind her that he's not a good guy.

"I'm willing to forgive him for that."

"Oh, you are?" I say sarcastically. "What a loyal best friend."

"Oh, please. Your ego is more bruised than your wrists," Rune says as we cross the street. "And your backpack only has minor banana-peel damage. Admit it—you're mad because he stood up to you and won."

"He did *not* win anything!"

"If you say so."

"I do."

"Then I believe you." But I know she doesn't.

We don't say anything for a block. When we stop at a crosswalk, waiting for traffic to pass, Rune studies me with an odd expression. "I should have been more supportive. Sorry."

"You should be—supportive *and* sorry."

She gestures to my jeans. "I never liked those jeans anyway. Let's hit the thrift stores and find some seventies bell bottoms. My treat for being a sucky BFF."

"Thanks." I offer a small smile. "And you don't suck. It's my whole day that sucks. I shouldn't take it out on you."

"You shouldn't," she agrees. "But friends should support each other and I'm always here for you. I hope you'd do the same for me."

"Always," I promise.

"Even if I ask a favor that you won't like?"

My silver bangles jingle as I fold my arms across my chest, eyeing her suspiciously. "Depends on what you're asking."

"This might make you mad, but I have to know."

"What?"

"Would you recognize his voice?" By the hero worship in her tone, I know exactly who she's talking about. I'm disgusted she's so obsessed with this guy, but she's my friend and I did promise to be supportive.

I think for a moment, then nod. "Yeah. I won't forget his voice." *Or forgive him*, I vow to myself.

"So, if you hear his voice again and figure out who he is, you'll tell me?" Rune's practically begging. "Please."

"Well…yeah." I shrug. "I'll tell you."

Then she grins—so sappy and silly I want to hurl—and I realize she'll want me to listen to every guy at school until I find the Grin Reaper.

It's not such a bad idea, I decide, but for a completely different reason.

When I find the Grin Reaper, I'll reap my own justice. He won't need to hide behind a mask, a concealing jacket, and gloves anymore. I'll make sure everyone at school knows exactly who he is—his admirers and his enemies.

Revenge.

FIVE

I drop Rune off at her house and continue on to mine.

Not that I want to go home. More than anything, I long to climb on a bus and return to Sheridan Valley, maybe hide out at my friend Sabine's house until I graduate high school and can live my own life.

Dread twines through me like a taut rope, tugging in different directions. I have to go home; I don't want to go home. I want to be honest; I can't tell the truth. I need to be myself; my family needs me to be someone else.

It's not the wrath of Mr. Sproat or even the weird necklace that worries me.

It's the crumbled paper at the bottom of my backpack.

The letter.

When I saw my name in the first line, I got a sick feeling. But it was the last paragraph that shot fear through me, as if by reading it I'd unleashed a Pandora's box of evils on the world.

On my family.

There's no closing the lid once truth is uncovered. I think of lame sayings like "knowledge is power" and "ignorance is bliss." I'd give anything for blissful ignorance instead of knowing what's written in there. Even more, I wish my parents didn't know. How can I face them? I think the letter must have arrived yesterday, given the date on it, but Mom worked late at the church so there wasn't a chance to talk. Are my parents waiting until after dinner tonight, to talk to me alone? Or will they confront me when I walk into the house? I don't want to hurt them ... but I don't want to change who I am, either.

I leave the sidewalk for a graveled road that leads to an older section of Nevada Bluff, then up a steep hill to the few farm houses that belonged to the original residents of the town. Perched on the top of the hill is our white three-story house. It's not much to look at, and the plumbing is so ancient you have to flush twice. There's no dishwasher, which is a tragedy in a house with six kids—well, seven kids if you count K.C., who sleeps in a room over the garage.

The wooden gate creaks as I enter the yard, setting off the yapping of Mom's pom-poo Sassy. Her barking sets off shouts of "Quiet, Sassy!" from inside the house. I recognize Dad's voice and nerves knot in my stomach.

Avoidance is my best—my only—defense. So I sneak around to the back and reach into thick ivy for the almost invisible string that dangles from my third story balcony. I yank on the string and a roll of fabric tumbles down into my hands. It's a silken ladder, originally from Japan, but a great find in an antique shop for $4.99.

A secret back way into the house.

I climb up the swaying ladder, balancing carefully so I don't fall. When I reach the balcony, I grasp the rail and heave myself over onto the wooden deck, which is old and in need of a paint job like the rest of the house. But the third floor is blissfully all mine. For the first time in my life I have a room to myself—practically a suite, with a large bedroom and kitchenette and bathroom. There's no closet, only a large wardrobe, which is fine with me since it's the reason my three sisters chose rooms on the second floor. My twin brothers are only five, so they share a room on the ground floor near my parents. And K.C. has a private apartment in the backyard garage.

I roll the ladder back up and dangle the string down into the ivy before I go inside and toss my backpack on the floor. I stare at it for long minutes before finding the courage to reach inside for the letter. My parents are sure to come to me tonight for a grave discussion and I need to be prepared.

Dear Minister Matthews,

I'm writing to discuss the serious and alarming matter of your eldest daughter. As a parishioner of your church, I admire your dedication and hard work, but I am very concerned about Beth Ann. I am in close contact with teachers at Nevada Bluff High, so I am aware of the truth of her behavior. The issue is not only her shocking appearance, but her consistently rude treatment of authority figures as well as her classmates.

She is a poor reflection on her parents—and on the Church of Everlasting Hope.

Beth Ann, who insists on going by the crude name of Thorn, disregards rules and is in danger of failing at least one of her classes. She only associates with disorderly students. Her contempt for other students is evident in her refusal to volunteer for campus organizations.

If I did not have such high respect for you, Minister Matthews, I would go straight to the Church's board of directors with my concerns. But as a parent, I realize it's a challenge to control a difficult teen. Still, you must control Beth Ann before irrevocable damage is done to your reputation and, by association, to the reputation of the church and its members.

If Beth Ann's behavior continues on its deteriorating course, I will have no choice but to recommend that the Church board of directors find a new minister. I would deeply regret having to do this, but it will be my duty.

Sincerely, Your Concerned Friend

The anonymous signature is a mask hiding a coward's identity. The letter writer is no friend of my mother's; it's a bully wielding threats instead of fists. And the threat is clear. Either I give up everything goth, including my friends, or my mother loses her job. And with Dad out of work, Mom is the sole support for our large family.

There's a knock at my door.

I shove the letter into my sock drawer and brace myself to face the wrath of "concerned" parents. Dad's been ill-tempered anyway since losing his job and makes no secret that he doesn't approve of me. But Mom prides herself on being fair and says I'm free to express myself. Although she forbids tattoos, she was cool about my pierced tongue, belly button, and eyebrow.

Still, with her job at stake, can she afford to be fair?

"Thorn. You in there?"

Not Mom or Dad. Thank God.

I release the breath I've been holding and jump up to open the door for my honorary brother, K.C.

K.C. wipes his hands on his grease-stained overalls and waits for me to invite him in before entering my room. Although taller than me, he seems shorter, his shoulders slightly hunched as if wary of the world. He's a gentle soul, average and overlooked in shades of brown and quiet. After having had some bad breaks, he's my mother's latest do-good project.

"Where were you at lunch today?" he asks as I shut the door behind him. "I waited on the steps, but you never showed."

I bristle because I don't owe him an explanation. But his tone isn't angry or critical, just curious. His brown eyes are wide with trust, and I feel a bit guilty for ditching him. It wasn't intentional. I just totally forgot.

"Sorry, K.C.," I say as I pick up my guitar out of habit and sit at the edge of my bed. I gesture for him to sit beside me, but instead he pulls out a chair from my desk close to my bed. "Something came up with Amerie."

"The singing competition?" K.C. guesses. "I heard a wild rumor that Philippe was here, but who can believe something that ridiculous?"

"Believe it. Amerie met him."

"He's really going to be a judge?"

"Yeah. Amerie practically flew to the moon with excitement." The news about Philippe seems like it happened weeks ago. Weird to realize it was only this morning.

"What's a big star doing at our little school?"

"He used to go here. But it's just a publicity stunt." I hold my guitar tight and strum a few clashing chords. "I bet the principal gives him an honorary diploma even though he didn't graduate."

"I'd ask you if you're going to enter, but you'd probably smack me."

"No probably about it. Contests are an unfair measure of humanity and bring out the worst in people."

"Yeah, yeah … but they're fun, too," he says.

"Not interested." I curl my fingers around my guitar.

"Did you hear about the other excitement today?" K.C. asks, wisely switching the subject. "Bruce Gibson locked in the old gym?"

I hesitate, then nod. "Yeah, I heard. Rune called him 'Brute.'"

"Bruce's mother would have, too, if she'd known how

big and mean he'd turn out," K.C. jokes. "He was lucky to be found so quickly. I wouldn't want to get stuck in that creepy gym. How'd a wrestler over six feet tall get squeezed inside a locker anyway?"

"Not a regular locker, an equipment locker," I say, before realizing I might be giving myself away.

But K.C. just nods. "Bruce deserved it after picking on that freshman. Always going after easy targets. I say justice was served for once. It's great the Grin Reaper is back."

"You sound like you knew about him before today."

"Who hasn't?"

I lift my hand.

"No way!" His jaw sags open.

"We've only been at Nevada Bluff a little over a month."

"So? You'd have to be dead and buried under a mountain of rocks not to hear about the Grin Reaper. Everyone's been wondering if he graduated or moved away. But it looks like he was just waiting for a good reason to strike." K.C. grins in a hero-worshipping way that makes me want to puke.

"Never trust anyone wearing a mask." I scowl at the purple-yellow bruise on my wrist. "If he was such a good guy, he wouldn't hide his identity."

"It's better if no one knows it. But that doesn't mean kids don't talk a lot, trying to guess who he might be."

"What have you heard?" I set aside my guitar and lean closer. K.C.'s talent for blending into the background unnoticed means he learns interesting things.

"The Reaper is a junior or senior, a rule-breaker, and

cuts class a lot. He probably has identifying marks or jewelry on his hands, since he hides them in gloves."

"That describes half the guys at school—even you."

K.C. lifts his hands. "No tattoos or rings."

"But you have a scar there." I point at his thumb knuckle. "And you usually have grease under your fingernails from working on cars. Hands give away a lot."

"So the Reaper is smart to hide his hands, or his secret would be out and he couldn't help anyone." K.C. glances toward the balcony window at the endless gray-blue sky. "I wish I had the guts to do what he does."

"Kidnapping, assault, and public humiliation? That's not bravery, that's brutality," I scoff, annoyed. "The guy isn't any better than his victims."

"But he does it for justice." K.C. tilts his dark head at me. "Like Spiderman or Robin Hood. I thought you'd respect him, since he's breaking rules to help people."

"By hurting others," I point out. Then I tense because I hear voices coming from downstairs. "Who's home?"

"Only your father and Amy."

Dad hardly ever goes out, holing up in his "office" and saying he's researching the job market. But Amy, a popular seventh grader, is always busy and so studious she makes Hermione Granger look like a slacker.

"Your mom drove the kids—except Amy because she's doing an extra credit project—to church for a Youth Group meeting," K.C. explains.

"Oh, yeah, it's Wednesday." Mom urged me to join the church's weekly Youth Group but I refused. I read metaphysical and theological books and have deep discussions (sometimes arguments) with Rune, so that's enough religion for me.

At least with Mom gone, I have a reprieve. But when she returns, I know she and Dad will call me in for a "talk."

Running off to California is sounding better all the time.

"You're looking serious, Thorn," K.C. says. "Something wrong?"

"Frequently." I give a wry grin. "But nothing I can't handle."

"Okay, don't tell me," he says with an understanding look. It's weird how he gets me, like he's more of a brother than my blood brothers. Of course, Alcott and Larry are only in kindergarten. "Still, if you, well, need anything, I'm here."

"Thanks, but you've got enough going on with school and the auto shop. Speaking of which, don't you have to go work on some cars about now?"

He glances at his watch. "Shit. Yeah."

Then he jumps up, bumping into my backpack which I'd left on the edge of my desk. My backpack tumbles to the floor and the golden-heart necklace rolls out.

When K.C. bends down to pick it up, a wild panic comes over me and I lunge down, grabbing the necklace.

"What's that?" K.C. asks, wrinkling his brow.

"Just a necklace I found at school," I say as I curl it in my palm, where it's as soft and cool as a caress. "You better hurry or you'll be late."

"So you're keeping it?" He gestures to the necklace.

"No." I shake my head firmly, as if trying to convince myself. "Definitely not."

"You want help finding the owner?" K.C. offers. "I can get up early tomorrow to make a flyer to post around school."

"For an ugly necklace?" I snort. "I don't think so."

"It's not that ugly. It looks interesting. Can I see it?"

I try to think of a reason to refuse, but come up blank. So I hand it over to K.C. My hand feels empty and cold. I fight an urge to snatch the necklace back.

He holds it by the shoelace, squinting at the shiny yellow pendant. "There's something written on the back."

"No way," I insist, but when I look closely, I notice faint markings. How did I miss it before? "Can you read it?"

"No." He pushes brown hair from his forehead as he concentrates. "A, J, and M or N. I'll need a magnifying glass to see more. Have you opened it yet?"

"Opened it? What are you talking about?"

"It's a locket. See the seam here?" He points to what looks like a scratch in the yellow paint. "There must be some mechanism to pop it open."

Watching him mess with my necklace irritates me. I grab it from him. If there's something hidden inside, I'll find out on my own. "I'll do it later."

"But I can help."

"I'll figure it out on my own. And you're going to be late if you don't leave now."

"Fine," he says, and by his tone I can tell I've pushed too far. He slams the door on his way out without saying good-bye.

I'm glad he's gone. I rub my fingers over the curved heart pendant... or I guess I should call it a locket. Does that imply something is "locked" inside? A precious memento of undying love, like a dried rose petal or tiny photo? Or more likely, K.C. is wrong and it isn't hollow.

But I can't stop wondering, so I snap on the light over my desk. I hold the locket under the bright yellow bulb, twisting it at different angles until I see a faint indentation. My finger slides over the groove and I dig my purple-tipped nail inside, jabbing and twisting until I hear a click.

The locket splits into two halves and swings open.

I stare in astonishment as a silky black curl falls into my hand. I hear a plaintive cry that sounds as far away as a moment lost in time. I think of the sarcophagus and death closing in. My chest tightens with horror.

And I know with certainty this curl was cut from a dead body.

SIX

I return the curl to the locket, but the soft touch of the fine hair lingers on my fingertips like a ghost impression. Who did it belong to? What happened? A tragedy, I'm sure of that, although that flash of connection is already fading like waking up from a bad dream. Still, the certainty of death is so strong that my heart is haunted by half-remembered grief. I have to know more.

I phone the one person who might be able to tell me.

Sabine answers right away.

"Thorn!" she exclaims before I even utter a word. Her voice is so sincere and warm that I ache for my life in California, and the friends I left behind even more.

"How did you know it was me?" I ask. "A psychic vision?"

"Caller ID." Sabine laughs.

I want to laugh with her but I'm staring down at the locket. Suddenly, I'm reluctant to talk about it, which makes no sense. Sabine will totally understand. She comes from a long line of psychics and has been seeing ghosts since she was a little girl. Her predictions are scary accurate. If this locket is haunted, she'll know.

"Thorn, are you still there?"

"Yeah. It's just … "

"Are you okay? I'm getting a strange vibe, like you want to ask me something but there's a wall between us. And you're holding something that glows like a golden egg, only it's dangerous like a grenade. Does any of this make sense to you?"

"Yeah." I glare down at the locket and think, *You have no control over me!* "Sabine, I've been having strange feelings and visions since I found a locket. It's messing with my thoughts and freaking me out."

"I've heard of things like this happening with old jewelry. Nona says antique jewelry can hold onto energy from its previous owners. Remember all the trouble I had with that antique witch ball?"

"Yeah—but this locket isn't very old or possessed by an evil spirit. It's cheap and tacky, with a shoelace instead of a chain."

"Hmmm … there's weird energy around you."

I swallow. "A … a ghost?"

"Not exactly, but something supernatural. I can feel it."

"You can? Even when we're like two hundred miles apart?"

"Psychic vibes are sort of like phone lines. We don't have to be physically together for our energy to connect," Sabine says. "Tell me more about the necklace."

"I found it on the stage in the auditorium," I begin,

then explain how there had been chaos on stage because of Philippe's sudden visit and I have no idea who lost the locket.

"*The* Philippe?" Sabine gives a fan-girl squeal. "As in super-star rocker?"

"Down, girl," I tease. "He was here, but I didn't see him so I can't tell you much except someone on the stage with him lost the locket. And when I opened it, I found..."

"What?" she asks after I hesitate.

"A curl of soft black hair."

"I just got shivers up my arms," Sabine says.

"It gave me the creeps, too. I'm sure it was cut from someone who was dead," I add grimly. "I don't know why I'm so certain of this, but I know it's true."

"You're psychic, Thorn, that's why you know."

"Stop already. I just find things—like this damned locket. You're the one who sees ghosts and talks to your spirit guide. Can you see anything now about the locket and curl?"

"I'm closing my eyes and concentrating... this may take a minute." The phone goes silent and all I hear is my own quick-thumping heart. When Sabine comes back on, her voice is whispery. "I can't see anything, but I smell damp dirt."

"Like a grave?" I guess, shivers rippling down my arms, too.

"Maybe. I'll try contacting my spirit guide. It takes some concentration—for an entity over three hundred years old, Opal can be stubborn. But she knows a lot."

In the subsequent silence, I visualize Sabine in her attic bedroom with its homespun lavender décor... the quilt on the bed and the stained glass window. Whenever Sabine is thinking, she twirls the black streak in her blond hair that she says is the mark of a Seer. I twist my hair, too, hoping she'll come up with answers so I can free myself of this strange obsession with the locket.

"My spirit guide wasn't much help," she finally says with a sigh. "Opal says confusing things that are hard to understand. I'll try to repeat it, although it doesn't make sense. She said, 'A broken melody bleeds betrayal. Long-buried truths will be uncovered when the Finder follows the map.'"

"What map?"

"All Opal would tell me is that the map rides a paper saddle."

"That doesn't make sense."

"Exactly. Way confusing." Sabine sighs. "When I asked Opal to translate it into English, she got all huffy and left. I'm sure she meant you when she said 'the Finder.' Maybe her words will mean something to you later."

"Maybe," I say, disappointed.

Sabine asks about my family, and I'm glad to change the subject so I catch her up on Mom's job, my siblings, and K.C. When she asks about school, I share some of Rune's *Weird News* stories like space debris splashing into a wedding cake, and a twenty-foot-tall cornstalk.

I purposely avoid talking about the Grin Reaper.

Sabine fills me in on our mutual friend, Penny-Love, who is always at the center of some romantic drama. Her latest drama involves three new boyfriends who don't know about each other.

"What about *your* boyfriend?" I ask Sabine.

"Dominic is great." Her voice softens. "His farrier business is keeping him super busy."

"Too busy for you?"

"Never. We schedule a date night at least once a week."

"I'm glad. You two are like the perfect couple," I say enviously. I wonder what it would feel like to love someone so much—and have him love me back.

When we hang up, I'm empty and aching inside. I miss Sabine and my old life, but it's deeper than that. I have a sense of foreboding, like a dark wind is sweeping me toward the edge of a steep cliff and I may not survive the fall.

The locket taunts me. I have no idea what map to follow. How am I supposed to know what that means? The closest thing to a map in my room is a basketball-sized globe on my desk. I flick a finger at the globe and watch it spin. My vision blurs as I wait for magic to happen. But nothing does.

I cross over to my trash can and dangle the locket, tempted to toss it away forever.

But once again, I can't.

I try to push the locket out of my mind. I open a book that Rune loaned me, *Candle Burning Rituals: Spells for Every Purpose.* I can't find any spells for dealing with haunted lockets, so I perform a basic spell warding off dark spirits. I gather red votive candles, an athame (sharp pin), smooth rocks, anointing oil, and herbs. I arrange them on an altar (end table), then anoint the candles with oil. I sprinkle the herbs at the base of the candles, then set the stones facing south to increase energy. I murmur words that I don't under-stand, but which sound very mysterious, as I use the athame to carve words of protection into the candles.

When I finish, I blow out the candles and close the spell book.

Doors bang. Voices rise from downstairs. Mom is back from church.

But Mom doesn't come to my room. *What's going on?* Are my parents waiting till after dinner to confront me about the letter? I mentally rehearse my defense, pointing out that it's unfair to punish me because of one bitchy person. My grades (except for History) aren't *that* bad. And no one has the right to criticize my friends.

All through dinner, I'm on my best behavior. I say "please" and "thank you," even to the twins who just grab what they want, even if it's on my plate. And when my youngest sister Meg spills milk in my mashed potatoes, I don't slap her.

I wait and wait, wondering when the accusations will come.

Only they never do.

That night I'm tormented by uneasy dreams, in which squiggly lines curve and shape into roads that lead nowhere and I'm lost in a nightmare fog of despair. The next morn-ing, I take a look in the mirror and groan at the dark circles under my eyes. I won't need much makeup to look like a ghoul today.

I glance over at my wig shelf, debating which one to wear. I'd dye my hair like most goths except for my weird allergy to hair dye. My natural hair is a drab dark-blond and makes me look like I'm twelve instead of seventeen, so wigs aren't a choice but a necessity. I choose a spiked, devil-red one.

Next comes my three-step routine:

Step 1: I smooth on a pale ivory foundation, around my face and down my neck. Instead of concealing my black circles, I exaggerate them, smearing on velvet-black eye shadow for hollow "dead" look. Then I slash a bruise of blood-red blush down my cheek. Black eye-pencil darkens my blond brows. And my lips bleed red gloss inside a dark outline of midnight black.

Step 2: I choose jewelry, putting studs in my eyebrows and multipierced ears. Metal chains go around my neck, beaded bracelets dangle on my wrists, and rings glimmer on my fingers. I add an ankle bracelet that looks like prison leg-cuffs. Very cool find for just $3.25 at a yard sale.

Step 3: Clothes always take longer, since I have a large wardrobe closet crammed with skirts, blouses, vests, jackets, belts, tights, corsets, leggings, and scarves. Then there are the shoes. Getting the right look is a fine art. I belt my favorite black velvet skirt and a laced black shirt, and wear a large red cross over my breasts.

I feel like myself... on the outside, anyway.

At breakfast, I avoid squabbling with my sibs and pretend not to notice my father's frown when he sees me. Dad doesn't complain, at least not anymore. But he doesn't approve, either. Mom is cool, even going thrift-store shopping with me a few times. The wig I'm wearing was her gift for my seven-teenth birthday.

But that was long before the letter.

And still they don't mention it to me.

———————

I've avoided conflict at home, but not at school.

When I walk into homeroom, my science teacher Mr. O'Brien hands me a note—a summons to the principal's office.

No reason to stress, I tell myself. It's not the first time I've gone to a principal's office—although it's the first time at Nevada Bluff High.

Principal Niphai is a soft-spoken man who wears a col-orful golf shirt and collects assorted golf balls on his desk in a dish, the way some teachers keep candy. He barely glances up at me, one hand tossing a blue-striped golf ball while he flips through papers with the other.

"Mr. Sproat says you cut his class yesterday."

"Not the whole period," I reply, trying to keep the sar-casm to a low minimum. Despite what some people think, I don't intentionally piss off authority figures—unless they deserve it.

"But you did leave and not return?"

"Um … yeah."

"Do you want to tell me why?"

"Not really."

"So you have no excuse?"

"Not really."

"That makes this easy." He marks something off on a paper, his tone not really interested. "Detention. Today after school."

I hustle back to my class, relieved to escape without expulsion or a phone call to my parents.

"Bummer," Rune says when I tell her about my detention at lunch. We're back to our usual place on the steps behind the cafeteria. It's shady and private, but kind of stinky because of the nearby Dumpster.

"Detention isn't that bad."

"But you won't be able to walk home with me," Rune complains.

"Unless you want detention, too. I can help you break some rules," I offer, because she's my best friend and I'm willing to help her out.

"Not a chance!" Rune opens her bag lunch, then glances up. "K.C. can walk home with me," she says as he heads toward us.

"Where's Amerie?" K.C. asks. He sits on the stair step below me.

"Singing Star contest," I say with a roll of my eyes. "Good news, though—they reached the max number of entrants, so registration is closed and Amerie won't nag us to enter anymore."

"Supreme news!" Rune high-fives me. "I'm over Philippe anyway. Sure, he's hot, but his music is lame. Enough idiots around here act gaga over Philippe. I'd rather meet the Grin Reaper."

I glance down at my ham and Swiss sandwich, ignoring the look Rune gives me. She doesn't have to say it, but I can tell she still expects me to listen to the voice of every guy at school until I can identity the Grin Reaper for her. So I change the subject. "Hey, Rune, what's the weird fact for today?"

"A museum in Houston paid people twenty-five cents each to bring in cockroaches."

"Cool," K.C. mumbles, chewing an apple slice.

"That's just stupid," I say.

"But strangely true." Rune grins. "The museum plans to exhibit cockroaches feeding off decaying organic matter. If they weren't around, there would be more trash."

"Makes sense," K.C. says as he crumples a baggie. "But the museum people wasted a lot of money buying bugs that people would give them for free."

"Roaches are disgusting," I say.

"Vampires would love them." Rune spikes a cherry tomato from her salad with a plastic fork.

"How can you say that? Vampires are not carnivores," I remind her. "We've already argued that topic to death. They don't eat meat."

"But they drink blood—which drips from fresh meat." Rune puts down her fork. "Besides, I didn't say a vampire would eat a cockroach. Roaches have no blood vessels, so blood sloshes freely in their bodies. A vampire could stick in a straw and drink up."

"A roach slushie! Anyone got a straw and a roach?" K.C. says, which makes us all laugh.

Even through my laughter, a worry ticks within me as my internal clock warns that in just over an hour, I'll have to face my history teacher. And while Principal Niphai was cool, Mr. Sproat definitely won't be.

My prediction is dead-on right.

Mr. Sproat calls me to the front of the class and asks me to match each major war to the U.S. president at that time. Of course, he knows I don't know. I admit this and he gives me a look like I'm the stupidest student in the world. Then he assigns extra homework for the whole class, evilly shifting the blame onto me. When the bell rings, my classmates swear and shove, and one crude guy even spits on my boot.

When I show up for detention, my English teacher Ms. Chu is the not-so-lucky teacher assigned guard duty this week. I look around and count seven other students: five guys and two girls. I head for a desk away from everyone else until I get a thought that changes my direction: detention may be punishment, but it could also prove very educational—and I don't mean in a book-learning way. I remember K.C. saying the Grin Reaper is a habitual rule breaker.

And I stare at the five guys serving detention, wondering. Is one of them the Grin Reaper?

SEVEN

"Sit down, Thorn," Ms. Chu says with a smile. She's cool for a teacher, twenty-something with purple streaks in her super-short, bleached-blond hair.

"Sure, Ms. Chu." I nod at her, but my gaze still sweeps from guy to guy.

"Pick any seat, then pull out homework to do quietly for the next hour."

"And if I don't have any homework?"

"The white board needs to be cleaned."

"Just remembered some assigned reading," I say quickly.

I scoot into a seat beside a shaved-head guy with mocha skin and a ruby ring on his pinky that sparkles too brightly to be authentic. He's camouflaged in a baggy black jacket and hunched over a book, so I can't tell if he's ripped with rock-hard muscles or flabby like a dough boy.

When I stare at Shaved Head, he glances up at me, his dark-chocolate eyes flaring with something that could either be curiosity or annoyance.

"You come here often?" I ask, like I'm making a joke. All I care about, though, is hearing his voice.

He rolls his eyes like that's the stupidest question ever uttered in the universe, then calls me a name that would shock even Rune. He returns his attention to the graphic novel hidden covertly inside his textbook.

Rude jerk! I think of all the words I want to call him. But he's not worth my breath. Besides, I found out what I wanted. His voice is definitely not the Reaper's.

I contemplate the four other guys in the room. They're familiar in a seen-around-school way but I don't know their names. One is young, with a boyish face that won't see stubble for a few years, so I figure he's a freshman. There's a skinny guy with hair springing out all over, like he's feral, but he has blue eyes. Another guy is about the right age, but he's stocky and missing a neck.

I scratch them off my mental "Reaper" list.

Swiveling to my right, I shift my interest to the last guy, and am unable to take my gaze off the rattlesnake tattoo winding from his wrist up to his black-polished thumbnail. He looks older than a senior (held back a few times?).

He's a definite for my "Reaper" list. I appreciate his fine muscled shoulders, snug Levi's, and the snake design on his dark-brown western boots. But I also notice the royal blue jacket slung on the back of his chair. He's a Jay-Clone? Hard to believe, since he's wearing black nail polish. I'm intrigued, wondering if we're kindred rebels.

When Ms. Chu nails me with a stern frown and gestures

toward my book, I flip to a random page. But I'm sneaking glances sideways, thinking.

Rattlesnake Tat is muscular enough to have shoved me to the ground and stolen my backpack. But did he do it? He's definitely the type: intelligent with an edge of subversive, and tapping his boot like he has better things to do than waste time in detention. And he has a good reason to hide those black-painted fingernails in gloves.

Still, the real test is his voice.

Only how do I get him to talk? My oh-so-smooth attempt with Shaved Head completely bombed.

I consider slipping him a note. Only what would I say? I can't bluntly ask if he's the Reaper, and something like "Hi, I'm Thorn" would sound too lame. Worse, he might get the wrong idea and think I'm hitting on him—which is so not me. I have enough stress in my life without adding some guy. And even if I'm intrigued by his dark mysterious eyes and rebel vibe, he *could* be the Reaper. I glance down at the purplish bruises on my wrists and grit my teeth, determined. If he's the Reaper, he's going to pay for what he did to me. Call it justice or revenge. I won't only tell Rune his identity, I'll tell Amerie, which is like texting the news to every kid in Nevada.

Detention minutes are an anomaly of physics, moving slower than ordinary minutes. I'm so bored I actually read a chapter of my textbook. I look up at the clock, willing it to speed up. But time stops for all rule-breakers. I want to throw something to smash the stupid clock.

What I really want to do, though, is talk to Rattlesnake Tat.

Ms. Chu is busy on her cell phone and not watching me, so I purposely drop my pencil on the ground.

I swear under my breath like I'm annoyed with my own clumsiness.

My stealth pencil rolls right up to Rattlesnake Guy's foot. He glances down, then kicks the pencil back to me and grunts something like, "Hmmm."

"Thanks," I say softly, bending down to pick up the pencil.

"Hmmm," he says again, not looking at me.

"I'm Thorn. And you're ... ?"

Now he looks at me; dark brows knitting and a wisp of a smile curving into dimples. He glances over at the teacher's desk, then whispers, "Wiley."

I smile back, thinking of the Cartoon Channel my sibs torture me with. "Like the coyote?" I say.

He nods, but then looks away quickly as Ms. Chu calls out, "Thorn! No talking."

Damn, just when things are getting interesting.

"I dropped my pencil and was picking it up." I wave the pencil, my expression all innocence. "The tip broke off so I'll need to sharpen it."

I look hopefully at Wiley, willing him to loan me one. But he's returned to his book like I don't exist.

"You may use the sharpener," Ms. Chu says, gesturing toward the back of the room.

I walk down the aisle, replaying Wiley's voice in my head and trying to match it to the Reaper. But "Hmmm" and "Wiley" isn't much for comparison. And with Ms. Chu watching so closely, I won't be able to talk to him until after class—assuming he'll talk to me. He smiled and told me his name, but then turned away...was he afraid of getting in trouble, or was he avoiding talking to me because we've met before? Like yesterday in the haunted gym?

I poke my pencil in the sharpener, trying to figure out what to say to Wiley when detention ends. Dropping a pencil was too subtle; I should have dropped a book or my backpack (on his head). Okay, that was my hostility reacting. Seriously, to get him talking, I'll need a cool topic, maybe tats. Rune and I talk about them all the time and sometimes go into the only tat shop in town, Stuck For Life, and plan the tats we'll get when we turn eighteen.

The pencil sharpener buzzes till my lead tip is sharp.

On the way back to my desk (not in a hurry), I get a weird feeling as I pass a bulletin board covered with educational posters, student projects, and flyers. One flyer stops me. It's a promotion for a new arcade, offering discounts with a student ID. The flyer is cut into the shape of a saddle, and it shows a map of the town with directions to the arcade.

A map on a paper saddle—just like Sabine said.

I'm not thinking or even realizing what I'm doing when I lift my hands. It's like my brain is under siege by a compulsion to touch the map. My fingers reach out and the pencil in my other hand rises to meet the paper.

When my head clears, I'm standing in front of the saddle-shaped flyer with my pencil marking a spot on the map. I've penciled a large black X beyond the boundaries of Nevada Bluff, on a place called Stallion Creek.

From my fingertips to toes, I begin to shiver because I know this is the locket's way of leading me to answers, or perhaps of helping someone in trouble.

X marks the spot.

And I have to go there.

———————

Instead of waiting to talk to Wiley after Ms. Chu dismisses us, I grab my backpack, sling it over my shoulder, and jump out of my chair. With the image of the X blazing like a beacon in my head, I'm filled with an urgency that races along with me as I run down the walkway.

There's hardly anyone around, although as I pass the auditorium I hear singing. The Singing Star contest. I'm not interested until I realize that Amerie will be inside, and unlike me, she has her own car.

I push open a metal door, scan the auditorium, and see wings. Amerie stands on the stage talking to a thirty-something woman in a red business suit. Further back on the stage, surrounded by at least a dozen students and a hulky dude who I guess is a bodyguard, is Philippe—bronzed, tall, a wild black ponytail spiraling down his back.

My heart rushes, despite my logical brain reminding me that he's just another guy and being a super star doesn't make him special, any more than my finding things makes me special.

Still, he's really hot in snug jeans and a leather vest.

"Thorn!" Amerie lifts her arm to wave, her wings

glittering under the bright lights and giving the odd impression that she's taking off for a flight. She murmurs something to the red-suited woman, then hurries over to me. "I knew it!" she tells me triumphantly. "You couldn't resist coming to see Philippe!"

"Don't be dense. I'm so not interested."

"Really? Isn't that why you're here?"

"Not even close."

"Sure you wouldn't like an introduction?" Amerie asks with a wink of glitter lashes.

"What part of *not interested* didn't you understand? I am *not* a groupie."

"Stick around and you will be. Just don't get ridiculous like some of the other girls. Ruby is supposed to be interviewing contestants for the school newspaper but she's only flirting with Philippe. I finally had to warn her to act professionally or leave. But I can't blame her—he's so cool, and super nice, too."

"His fans can have him. I came to talk to you."

"Really?" She lights up like I've given her a gift. "About what?"

I hesitate, because Amerie worked hard to buy her car. She has personalized plates that say *FAREGRL* and speaks of her car like it's a real person. But I can't think of another way to get to Stallion Creek. So I flash the closest thing to a sweet smile ... then I beg.

And it works.

I must have said "please" a dozen times and promised to

be back in one hour. Amerie isn't happy about loaning *FARE-GRL* to me, but she's too nice to refuse a desperate friend.

So, with keys bouncing on a pink rhinestone Tinker Bell key ring, I hop in Amerie's car and follow the map that's fixed firmly in my head. I don't actually visualize the map; it's more a sense of directions and distances. The route is easy enough, and I have a way of finding places even if I'm given the wrong directions. I don't need street names; the black penciled X calls to me. And I can feel energy pulsating from the heart-shaped necklace in my backpack.

Still, I worry I'm doing something dumb. *Turn around and forget all about this*, I tell myself as I leave the school parking lot. But I keep driving, past the football field, and turn right onto a road that seems to disappear into the ragged, yellow-brown hills.

Based on the map, I know I'm supposed to go in this direction for about five miles, then wind through a canyon until I reach Stallion Creek. Then I'll make a left up and over a hill until I dip down into a valley. My internal map will let me know when to stop.

Amerie's car radio is fixed on a country station. The dash has so many buttons and dials that I can't figure out how to turn the music off, although I do manage to turn it down. But I can still hear the twangs and ballads of lost loves and heartbreak. A song about someone dying of a broken heart seems foreboding, as if the universe of Station KWIT is sending me a warning.

As the hills climb higher and thicken with wild brush, my uneasiness grows. No one knows where I am. I don't have a cell phone, since my family can barely afford the one Mom and Dad share. If I could call someone, I'd choose Sabine. I'd feel a lot better if I could hear her say I'm doing the right thing.

I slow when I see the Stallion Creek sign on a partially finished housing development. There are a few completed houses perched on a hillside with cars and signs of life, but on this eerie street wooden frames stick up like gravestones; houses that may never be homes.

A ghost neighborhood.

The only sign of life is a sheriff's car parked by a portable potty. Is he taking a break or patrolling the housing development? I slouch in my seat, not wanting to be noticed, and keep driving. When I reach a dirt road, I make a sharp left. Dust flies by my window and gravel rumbles beneath the tires. I cringe, knowing Amerie's car is getting filthy. I'll promise her a car wash when I'm finished here.

Finished doing what? I'm afraid to find out the answer.

After following a dried creek bed for over a mile, I pull off the side of the road by a lone oak tree, its limbs gnarled and a burn mark scarring its trunk. This is *it*. No way to explain how I know; I just know.

I step out of my car, into an icy wind that rips through the canyon and chills me to my bones. The terrain is rough—uneven, and with dips and rises that stretch beyond the hills. I feel small and not sure what I'm supposed to do now. Something has been calling to me, and since it all started with the locket, I dig into my backpack for it.

Is it my imagination, or is the locket shining as if glowing from the inside? How could I ever think it was ugly? It's golden and glorious. I caress it; it's so warm and alive, as if the heart is beating with life. When I slip the necklace on, I hear a plaintive cry—only it's not coming from the locket or inside my head, it's coming from the burnt tree.

The gnarled tree is tall and broken, as if abandoned by nature to a slow death. I move toward it cautiously, compelled by things I don't understand and afraid of what I'll find. I reach out with shaky fingers to touch the blackened trunk. I look from ground to branch, not sure what I'm supposed to find. There are no hidden holes or strange messages blazed into the bark.

"Why am I here?" I whisper to the golden heart that's resting against my chest.

I walk in a wide circle around the tree, and nearly trip over small piles of freshly dug dirt. There are also claw marks and paw prints. A wild animal, like a fox or coyote, was digging.

Curious, I bend over the hole. A scrap of blue fabric hangs out of it as if an animal had started to drag it away. A heat pulses through me and I reach down for the blue fabric, which is soft and shiny like satin. There's a faded design, too, in the dirt-crusted fabric … tiny animals of some kind. Elephants? Weird.

My finding radar is really off this time. No answers to the mystery of my locket; only garbage. Driving here was a waste of time, and I'm annoyed with myself for giving into freaky imaginings.

So I turn to leave, but pause when the sunset peeks from

beneath a cloud, shining golden-brown on the dirt-crusted twigs clinging to the blue rag. *Not a rag*, I realize as I bend down again, careful not to touch it. *A child's blanket*. And the twigs are shaped oddly; disconnected yet strangely symmetrical, like leathery beads once linked together. I lean closer, then draw back with a sharp intake of breath.

The twigs are not twigs.

They're human bones.

Tiny fingers.

EIGHT

All the air sucks out of me. Can't gasp or scream. Beyond horrified. Sick to my soul. My feet finally move. Running back to the car.

Why did I come here? I fumble for Amerie's keys. Warnings were there: the cries, the vision of a damp earth and danger. But I never thought I'd find... OMG. Those tiny fingers break my heart. I collapse against the side of the car. I want to run away and forget what I've seen. But powers larger than my own fears brought me here. I have to report this, so the tiny lost soul can find peace.

If I don't, I won't have any peace.

But reporting it means admitting that I came here because of a vision—which is unbelievable. When I can't offer a logical explanation, suspicion will fall on me. My family could suffer, too. I can't report what I found, but I can't pretend it never happened, either.

As I lean on the car, trying to decide what to do, I see bright lights flashing in my driver's side mirror.

I whirl around just as the sheriff's car pulls up beside me. The decision is out of my hands.

The sheriff is middle-aged, his dark-blue uniform stretched across his middle. He moves slowly, in the stereotypical manner of a country sheriff. Yet there's a sharp awareness in his face that's not at all small-town. He pushes up his cap, his gaze shifting over me and then narrowing in a familiar judging way. And when I catch a shadowy reflection of myself in the car window, I see what he's seeing: devil-red wig, corpse makeup, metal on my skin and clothes.

This isn't going to be easy.

He introduces himself as Sheriff Hart, then fixes me with a hard stare. "What are you doing way out here?"

My mouth opens but nothing comes out.

"Are you all right, miss?" he asks more kindly.

"I—I am ... but not that poor ... " I clench my chilled hands together. "I—I found ... found something."

He doesn't move, studying me. "What are you talking about?"

"Over there ... " I point, closing my eyes to shut out the image. "Behind the tree."

"Show me," he says with thick suspicion.

I shudder. "I—I can't."

His hand rests on the hilt of the gun at his side, studying me. Then he nods, as if coming to some decision. "Stay right here," he tells me. "Don't go anywhere."

"Okay," I murmur. My legs wobble and I lean against Amerie's car for support.

I watch him stride over to the burnt tree, his gaze sweeping around, on alert as if expecting an ambush. He stops abruptly, a few feet from the hole.

"What's this?" he calls over to me sharply. "Were you digging?"

"I—I wasn't."

"Could have been an animal." He bends down, rubbing his chin. "What's this?"

My stomach clenches and I know the exact moment when he's seen past the dirt and ragged cloth...to the tiny finger bones. An intake of breath. But he recovers quickly, backing away and brushing past me as he strides to his vehicle. I don't move, as instructed, but my mind drifts, so I'm only half-aware of the sheriff barking orders into a phone. It's not until he finishes talking and comes over to touch my shoulder that I snap back to this awful reality.

"How did you know to come here?" he asks, steel behind his words.

"I didn't know anything. I was just out driving."

"Do you have any idea what's over there?" He pointed past the burnt tree.

Tensing, I nod.

"So you'll understand why I need to get a statement from you."

I hesitate, then nod.

"We can't do that here, so I'll have to ask you to come to the station with me." There's underlying hostility in his tone, as if he's found me guilty and can't wait to lock me up. Freak goths are liars, right? I get that all the time. Sure, I lie sometimes, but not when it's important. Unfortunately, my truth is more unbelievable than any lie.

"I don't know anything," I insist. "I need to get home or my parents will worry."

"They should worry," he says. "May I see your driver's license?"

Not a question. An order.

I imagine the news headline: *Minster's Daughter Finds Grave Under Suspicious Circumstances*. No, I can't do that to Mom. She'll get fired for sure.

But I can't refuse the sheriff, so I hand over my license. It's a horrible picture, of me with blond hair and no makeup. My heart sinks like quicksand.

I shift in my army boots while the sheriff studies my license. He rubs his chin. He makes "hmm" sounds. Then he picks up a phone and steps away from me so I can't hear what he's saying.

Amerie's car keys dangle from my fingers, the tiny pink fairy wings sparkling as if ready to fly away. I wish I had wings.

"Beth Ann Matthews," the sheriff says, turning back toward me. "Why does Matthews sound so familiar?"

I shrug. "It's a common name."

He snaps his fingers. "Are you any relation to our new minister?"

I groan. Can things get any worse?

Of course they can.

———————

The next hour is forgettable—at least I'd like to forget.

Waiting on a hard plastic chair, strangers staring at me or ignoring me, conversations buzzing like white noise. I shut most of it out until Sheriff Hart informs me that my father is on his way.

Just great, I think miserably. Why couldn't it be Mom?

When Dad arrives, he avoids looking directly at me. He sits stiffly beside me while I answer questions.

Unfortunately, everything I say sounds wrong.

Sheriff Hart shoots off questions like his words are bullets and I'm standing in front of a firing squad. I think I'd prefer bullets. His questions rip through truth and lies so I hardly remember what I've said. I can't tell him about my finding or the curl hidden inside my locket. If they search me and find the curl (which I'm sure belonged to the buried baby), I might as well dig a grave for myself and dive in.

So I stick to a simple (lame) story about driving around randomly and noticing the dug-up area. "I thought an animal had been digging recently. I had no idea it was a grave...with baby bones..." I close my eyes tight to shut out the memory.

"Baby?" The sheriff's gray-brown brows arch with surprise as he leans forward in his chair, his jacket open slightly to give me an up-close-and-scary view of his gun. "We don't know for certain the bones are from an infant."

"It's a logical guess," Dad puts in. "We've moved here recently, so there's no way she could be involved in...well...whatever happened."

"Easy enough to prove through a DNA test," Sheriff Hart says.

That sounds worse that it turned out to be—just a quick cotton swab of my cheek.

Afterward, I touch the hidden locket under my shirt, aware that the real DNA is hidden inside it. At least that secret is safe ... for now.

I return Amerie's car. She left school a while ago so I drive it to her house. And she is *not* happy with me. I hand over the Tinker Bell keys, profusely apologizing. I tell her I got lost in the hills and promise to make it up to her.

Dad has followed me in the family Waggoner. I fasten my seat belt and risk a glance up at his granite face.

"I'm sorry," I say softly.

"I'm sorry, too." Dad starts the car, then turns to look at me, frowning. "But even more, I'm disappointed."

His words drive a stake through my heart.

There's nothing I can say now, and he's not talking anyway. I wish I could explain, but he'd never believe that a locket psychically led me to a grave. Even though I didn't do anything wrong, suspicions will linger, rumors will spread. Mom could lose her job. Worse—she'll lose her trust in me. I've already lost Dad's.

I stare out the window, panicking inside. To prove my innocence, I need to discover what *really* happened to that baby. But my only clue is the locket. All I know about the person who lost the locket is that she was on the stage during registration for the Singing Star contest.

But with so many contestants, how can I find out which girl?

I can only think of one way.

Enter the singing contest.

NINE

Dinner that night is marred with avoidance and uneasy silences. Mom barely speaks to me and Dad completely ignores me. My sibs talk and argue and make enough noise that anyone watching would think we were a happy family. Maybe we were once, but not any more. And if Mom loses her job, I don't know how we'll survive.

When I'm alone in my room, I ache inside and wish crying came easy. I'm not one of those girls who can wash away misery with tears. Instead I reach for the comfort of my guitar, caressing the sleek molded wood of my old friend. I strum a few chords of a song I've been working, trying different combinations that don't work. Again and again, the melody starts off slow and bluesy but then the notes falter and it's all messed up.

Frustrated, I put away my guitar and go to bed early.

Sometime after midnight I wake up, tormented by nightmares of skeletons chasing me. My heart's racing and I glance around to make sure my nightmares aren't real.

I reach out for a lamp and the light flashes on so bright I squint, then my vision adjusts. There are no boogie monsters lurking in the corners. Still, I can't sleep, so I self-prescribe a cup of hot chocolate with marshmallows. But on my way to the kitchen, I hear raised voices and pause outside my parents' bedroom. They're arguing…about me.

"—didn't have anything to do with the unfortunate child," Mom says angrily. "Have a little faith in your daughter."

"You have too much faith," Dad retorts. "I know she was lying. She didn't just accidentally find that grave—she knew where to look."

"You can't think she had anything to do with it!"

"Of course not. And the sheriff suspects the bones are six to eight months old. It's obvious what's going on with Thorn—she's covering for a friend."

"Perhaps," Mom says after a long pause. "But what if her story is true?"

"That she randomly drove to a remote hill and just happened to find a grave?" Dad scoffs. "I don't think so."

"Beth Ann always did have a knack for finding things," Mom says, calling me by my birth name although I've corrected her a zillion times. "Remember when she was five and she pointed to a poster for a lost dog and said the dog was locked in a garage? She cried so hard that I finally called the dog's owner and was told the dog had just been rescued from a neighbor's garage. I don't know how Beth Ann knew—she just did."

"You're making excuses for her. She's secretive and never

introduces us to her friends. She refuses to go to church with our family, which sets a bad example for the younger kids, and other people are noticing her behavior, too. Don't forget the letter."

"I refuse to pay attention to anonymous letters."

"Well, you should. You could lose your job."

"It's better than losing my daughter."

"We lost Beth Ann a long time ago." I hear a smack like Dad has hit his fist on a dresser. "And I don't know what the hell to do with Thorn."

I can't stand it anymore. Instead of going to the kitchen, I retreat back to my room. I'm shaking as I close the door behind me. I knew Dad disapproved of me, but I had no idea how much. He doesn't trust me…he doesn't even like me.

And it's not just about what happened to today. His resentment started before the letter, before we moved here—about the time he got laid off and took over carpooling, cleaning, and cooking while Mom worked longer hours. At first Dad just made snarky comments—"lighten up on the makeup" or "your natural hair would look better"—which pissed me off, so I avoided him. Somewhere over the summer, with moving and disappointments, we stopped talking.

I reach for my guitar; not to play, just to hold in my arms. It's a very long time before I fall asleep.

On the drive to school, K.C. sneaks curious glances at me like he suspects something is wrong. "Why are you so quiet?"

"Am I?" I shrug, avoiding his gaze.

"What's the weirdness with you and your parents? You're all so polite, yet not talking to each other. Your mom looked like she'd been crying."

"You're imagining things."

We reach the school parking lot and I jump out before K.C. can ask more. He's too perceptive for my own good.

Instead of meeting Rune at my locker, I search for Amerie in the auditorium. She's not there, so I try her homeroom class.

The warning bell will ring soon and the crowded walkways explode with noise and rushing. Most kids are headed to class, but I spot five guys in blue letter jackets clustered at an intersection. They're like fashion-magazine models, with gelled hair and expensive clothes and sneakers. They surround their idol, Jay Blankenship, whose golden-blond hair is jelled into perfect waves. His smug way of leaning back and lifting his chin when he talks makes him look tall, although he's under six feet. But it's the tallest Jay-Clone—with the snake tattoo and black fingernails—that I notice.

Wiley from detention.

He wears the blue letter jacket like the other clones but his tough attitude, black polish, and snake tattoo make him stand him out. My dad wouldn't approve of Wiley. If we dated, he'd have to sneak up my rope ladder to see me. Then I'll offer him my favorite tiny bottle—glittery black nail polish. We'd curl up on the couch, taking turns polishing each other's fingers and toes.

Wiley catches my gaze and, shock of shocks, grins. A

nice half-crooked smile, with just enough imperfection to show he's not completely boringly perfect like the other Jay-Clones. What is he doing with these preps, anyway?

I grin back, glad he can't read my mind.

Wiley turns away from his group, giving me a *come over* gesture.

Sure, why not? I can find out if he really is the Reaper. And if he isn't, there's always that bottle of black polish.

A group of basketball players, bouncing a ball between them as they hog the path, block my view of the Jay-Clones. But I hear one of them ask, "Who's the goth?" like I'm an object not a person. Snarky laughter follows until a different, startling familiar voice says, "Show some respect! She's the minister's daughter."

I jerk with shock, because I recognize that voice.

The Grin Reaper.

Wiley, I think excitedly. Although to be fair, I can't be sure it was his voice I heard; it could be any of the five guys.

From behind me I hear a rude shout—"Move it!"—and I'm shoved forward, pushed by the force of a crowd that's just heard the warning bell ring. When I break away, I look back but don't see the Jay-Clones.

Up ahead, though, I see Amerie.

Instead of wearing fluttery fairy wings, she has a silver, feathered headband swaying on her head like a winged halo. She's talking with three girls who look like seniors and are wearing gag-me-girly frothy peasant blouses, denim fringed skirts, and pink western hats. I hesitate, close to losing my nerve. For the first time since we met, I'm nervous about talking to Amerie. What I have to ask won't be easy.

"Hey, Amerie," I say, casual-like although my palms are starting to sweat. *Turn around now*, I urge myself, *before you completely lose your pride*.

"Why aren't you in homeroom?" Amerie's star earrings sway as she turns toward me. "Isn't it on the other side of campus?"

I shrug. "I have time."

"Cool." Amerie gestures to the frothy-pink-hat trio. "Thorn, these very talented girls are Micqui, Barbee, and Skarla. Their singing group is called the Cotton Candy Cowgirls."

"There were four of us before our guitarist quit, which sucks because we really need her," says the shortest cowgirl. "I'm Michelle, but everyone calls me Micqui." She didn't need to tell me that, since her name is written in pink letters on her ruffled blouse.

Freckled Barbee dips her pink hat and scowls down at me. She doesn't say anything, but I know she's checking out my gothness and thinking "freak."

"Barbee's my twin. Not identical twin, obviously," Micqui says. She sways as she talks, as if each word is choreographed to music only she can hear. "Barbee's hair is naturally a darker shade of brown than mine, although she hates me telling anyone she's not a real blonde. Is Thorn your real name? It's super cute."

And you're super annoying, I think, wanting to smack her for using the word "cute" on me. Instead I flash a fake smile. "Your costumes are so … um … colorful." *Like a candy store barfed.*

"Skarla put them together." Micqui proudly gestures to the third girl, who's wearing a huge grin and ginormous pink-rimmed glasses.

"The judges won't be able to miss your group," I say, and notice Barbee glaring at me like she knows I'm being sarcastic.

"Your costumes are gorgeous," Amerie says, shooting me a warning scowl.

"We don't usually wear them to school," Micqui adds.

"Really?" I feign surprise, as if this is news to me.

"Don't be silly," Micqui giggles. "It's for the contest."

"Presentation is important in any competition," Skarla says in her bubbly voice. She bounces forward. "We practice often and work hard to be our best. We'll only get one chance to make the finals, so we rehearse in costume to show the judges how professional we are and improve our chances for winning."

"I'm sure," I say with complete indifference. Enough time wasted humoring the chronically clueless. I lean in to whisper to Amerie. "Can we talk alone?"

"Now?" Amerie glances uneasily at her friends. "We weren't finished."

"I wouldn't ask if it wasn't important," I insist in a firm tone.

"Something up?" she whispers.

I nod. "I'll tell you about it in private."

Amerie's curiosity shifts into overdrive and she can't get

rid of her friends fast enough. Then she follows me down the path to a shadowed doorway.

"We won't be overheard here," I say.

"What is it? Have you met a hot guy? Are you finally going to hook up with someone?" she asks excitedly, obviously hoping for some juicy gossip.

"Nothing like that. Amerie, I need a favor."

"Oh, sure." She pats my hand. "Anything."

I bite my lip, unsure how to ask this. "I've changed my mind about the Singing Star contest."

"You no longer think it's subversive and anti-humanizing?"

"Not exactly." I suck in a bravery breath. "I—I want to enter."

"If this is your idea of a joke, I'm not laughing."

"Honest truth." My stomach knots. "I need to enter."

Amerie stares at me skeptically. "You'll go through auditions, criticism, judging, and getting up on a stage to sing in front of hundreds of people?"

Why does she have to put it like that?

"It may be my only chance to find out … um … if I have any talent." I grit my teeth. "Will you sign me up?"

"I'd love to—"

"Great!"

"—but I can't," she finishes.

My mouth falls open. "Why not?"

"I'm so sorry, Thorn. You waited too long." Amerie shakes her head miserably. "The contest registration is closed."

"You're in charge of the contest. You can get me in."

"It's not up to me," she insists. "Philippe's manager Collette is running the show. She's anal about rules."

"Please, Amerie. I really need to do this."

"Oh, Thorn, you're breaking my heart, but I can't help," Amerie says sadly. "I never in a zillion years thought you'd want to enter."

Disappointment slams into me. If this doesn't work, I'm out of ideas. I need to get up on stage with the other entrants to find out who lost the locket. Tight security will make it even harder. Not being in the contest will make it impossible.

"Isn't there some way you can get me in?" I beg.

Amerie taps her pink-frosted thumbnail on her chin, her expression changing as she thinks. She starts to say something, then closes her mouth and shakes her head. "You'd never do it."

I think of the buried bones, the sheriff's suspicious gaze, and the disappointment in Dad's voice. I have to find the owner of the locket.

"I'll do anything to get into the contest," I tell her.

"Anything?" Maybe it's my imagination, but her feathered halo seems to shimmer a warning shade of red. "There is one way, only you'll hate it."

"Just tell me," I insist.

So she tells me—and she's right.

I hate it.

TEN

If that's true, I'll drink a cockroach slushie," Rune says when I confess what I've done. We're lunching on the steps behind the cafeteria, where a faint aroma of ripe garbage always assures us of privacy. K.C. hasn't shown up yet today, and since Amerie is busy with the contest, it's just Rune and me.

"Serve up the cockroach." I hang my head. "I'm the new fourth member of the Cotton Candy Cowgirls."

Rune's dark eyes glitter angrily, as if I've betrayed something important between us. "Who *are* you? What have you done with the real Thorn?"

"I kidnapped her and she's locked in a trunk in the cellar."

"Seriously, Thorn." Rune stomps her high-top black boots on the lower step. "How did Amerie convince you to do this? Blackmail you with a horrible secret?"

"How else could I keep her from telling the world that I'm secretly a psycho mass murderer?"

"I'll mass murder you if you don't me why you really entered the contest."

"It's just something I need to do."

"But you hate contests."

I shrug. "Not so much any more."

She moves her bag lunch off her lap and looks deep into my eyes. "I can't believe you entered."

"Neither can I," I sigh.

"I won't lie and say I understand this insanity, but I'm your best friend and even if I don't like what you're doing, I'm all about support."

"Thanks," I say with a wry smile.

"I'll even go to the contest and applaud crazy loud when you win."

"Win? I don't think so." I shake my head. If things work out, I'll never even make it onto the stage.

"If you don't expect to win, why join such a ridiculous group? Excuse my gag reflex, but really, Thorn—*The Cotton Candy Cowgirls?*"

I cross and uncross my black-netted legs as if I can't get comfortable on the cement steps. I should have stuck with the psycho-killer story. A lie would be more believable than the truth. Now the best I can do is a half-truth.

"I'm just playing guitar and singing background. Amerie begged me to step in after their guitarist quit."

"You agreed as a favor to Amerie?" Rune's brows knit together like she's trying to wrap her brain about weird facts.

I shrug like it's no big deal. "You know how persuasive Amerie can be."

90

"Yeah. She usually gets what she wants. And who else can wear wings to school and get away with it? Teachers don't get on her case. Even the worst of the bullies leave her alone. Amerie is an unstoppable force of nature. But I don't think that's the real reason why you agreed to be in the contest."

"You don't?" I look down at the lunch I haven't opened, avoiding her gaze.

"Don't con me. You're using Amerie as an excuse because you love to play guitar and have been dying to enter the contest. I'm right, aren't I?"

"Well … music is important to me."

"I knew it." She lifts her energy drink as if congratulating herself.

I let her think she's right, although it bugs me that she believes I'd sell out my convictions. I want to assure her I'm still for individuality and against commercial corruption, but instead I ask her for her weird fact for today.

"A girl not much older than us was engaged to this amazing guy she totally loved and their future together looked great until her parents told her a horrible secret."

"That fifty percent of all marriages end in divorce?"

"Worse. That she'd been born a boy and she could never have kids."

"A boy? Wouldn't she know?" I glance down. "That's kind of hard to miss."

"Snip, snip." She pantomimes scissors cutting. "She had surgery as a baby and everything looked normal. How tragic—she never knew she wasn't completely a *she*. Can you imagine telling that secret to your boyfriend?"

91

I shake my head. "FYI, I don't have a boyfriend."

"Neither do I—although if you find the Reaper, I'm up for the challenge." She flashes me a wicked grin. "I'll let him know I'm all girl."

I grab my apple and take a bite, chewing so I conveniently don't have to reply. I refuse to get into an argument over that jerk Reaper.

Rune launches into another weird fact about an obscure South Pacific island where all the animals have multiple heads. *Humanity is so strange*, I think.

When I get to my Spanish class, the door is locked. Just great; Señor Rojas is running late again. Students gather by the door, waiting. Two girls I recognize from homeroom huddle close like they're telling secrets, only they're talking so loud everyone can hear. I'm not interested until I hear the word "bones."

My skin goes hot then cold. I step closer, listening.

" … that poor baby," I hear the chubby girl with braces say.

"How could anyone do something so hideous?" her friend replies, with a grim headshake that sends her long black ponytails flying.

"I can't even imagine! But I've heard that it's a girl from this school, only the sheriff can't release her name because she's a minor."

"No freaking way! Who could it be?"

"I don't know. But when she's arrested, we'll find out."

Señor Rojas arrives and they move their conversation

inside the class. I hang back, letting everyone else go in before following.

Rumors and whispers are already spreading. I should have known drama like a buried baby would get out. Not that anyone would connect it to me—at least not yet. But if the sheriff leaks my name, everyone will assume I know who did it even though I didn't live here when the baby died. "We knew she was bad news," kids will say. Adults will shake their heads and say how sorry they are for my parents. While I don't care who likes or dislikes me, I don't want to be the hot topic at school.

Finding the locket's owner is more urgent than ever.

I struggle through my last two classes, doing enough to get by. But I'm not really there. My thoughts are far away, on a deserted hill with small bones and the ragged remains of a baby blanket.

How did the baby die? Was it an accident?

Or murder.

I can't even go directly home after school since I have to meet the Cotton Candy Cowgirls for rehearsal. I enter the auditorium with the enthusiasm of someone walking to the guillotine. Off with my head, please. It would be less painful.

Noisy chaos explodes in the cavernous room. A swarm of excited kids (mostly girls, but I see a few guys too) surround the stage. Is Philippe up there? I strain my neck for a better look. The crowd shifts, and the figure at the center of the excitement is a pretty woman in her thirties waving a clipboard and barking out orders. The business manager Collette, I guess.

93

I'm hoping Amerie can introduce me to the girls who were on stage the day I found the locket. Only I don't see fairy wings anywhere. I do spot a trio of pink hats and sigh with resignation. Guillotine, here I come.

The pink trio welcomes me with fake smiles. They're as eager to work with me as I am to wear a pink western hat. Guess that makes us even.

"Where's your guitar?" Barbee asks.

"At home. I didn't know about all of this when I left the house this morning."

Micqui frowns. "How can we rehearse without music?"

"We can't," Barbee says. "It's like we're cursed. First Priscilla quits, and now we can't rehearse."

"Let's rehearse at my house," Skarla says, pushing between the sisters like a referee. "It'll be quieter there too, not noisy like here."

"With her in our group, we'll need extra rehearsals." Barbee turns to me. "We're scheduled to audition next Tuesday—that's only four days away! No offense, but that doesn't leave us much time to find a replacement if you suck."

"Or, you could suck. If you don't want me here—" I start to say.

"Of course we do!" Skarla intervenes, hooking her arm through mine like we're BFFs. "Amerie says you're really talented. That's so cool. Will you have any trouble meeting at my house at seven tonight? And be sure to bring your guitar."

Three stares under pink hats study me, like I've been given a test and they doubt I'll pass. *Whatever.*

I say I'll be there.

They leave the auditorium but I linger, gazing purposely around. The locket, which I've been wearing under my shirt, has grown warmer since I entered the room. It's uncomfortably hot now. Could it be sending me a message? That seems crazy even to me. Still, this is where it was found, so it makes sense the owner could be nearby.

So, instead of hiding the locket, I flaunt it around my neck. I hold the shoelace in a very obvious way, wiggling it so the golden heart jiggles above my breasts. *Everyone look!* I want to shout. A few do, but most are too busy singing or reading music or playing instruments. I run my fingers over the smooth locket and linger on the point, which is sharp but not enough to draw blood. I think of the fragile curl tucked inside and study the girls suspiciously. *Which one of you hid a pregnancy and then buried your secret in a shallow grave?*

But no one seems startled by the locket.

I'd ask Amerie to announce that a locket was found, except I don't see her anywhere. She's obsessed with this contest, so it's strange she'd leave early.

I leave, too, heading for the office to call K.C. for a ride home. But he doesn't answer his cell. Asking my parents is out of the question. Not because they'll refuse but for the opposite reason. Mom will be thrilled I'm involved in school activities and hanging out with "normal" girls—which is exactly why I won't tell her. Guess I'm walking home.

I'm passing the staff parking lot when I notice a ginormous, gleaming silver bus. Unlike the yellow clunk-mobiles students ride in, it's sleek and luxurious with reflective tinted windows glittering like mirrors. This has to be Philippe's tour bus.

My guess is confirmed when the door opens and automatic stairs unfold to the ground. Out steps gorgeous Philippe. And he's not alone. His arm is draped around the petite shoulders of a girl with light brown hair and some sort of sparkly hat on her head. No...not a hat. A winged headband!

Amerie? With Philippe?

Disbelief stuns me. Amerie never said anything about going out with Philippe. Not one word from the girl who usually spills volumes of gossip. I stare, even more shocked when Philippe stops to face Amerie and pulls her tight to his chest, his infamous long black curls spiraling over her shoulders as they embrace.

Are they kissing? Oh. My. God. Unbelievable!

I'm still gaping in shock as they stroll away, hand in hand, back toward campus, probably headed back to the auditorium.

Now I know why Amerie wasn't at rehearsal.

How did she work so fast? Sure, she admitted lusting after Philippe, and even I have to admit he's hot. But Amerie deserves a sweet guy who will cherish her, not someone who sold out creativity for commercialism. Amerie is selling out also, becoming a Philippe groupie. He's too old for her, too, and she's so gullible. He'll break her heart, and guess who will be left to pick up the pieces? This cannot end well.

I'm so lost in my thoughts that I almost miss movement by the silver bus. A shadowy figure creeps close to the tires.

Curious, I crouch down by an SUV to watch. The shadow pauses to furtively glance around, as if sensing he's being watched. He's draped in all black: long jacket, western boots, and a ski mask pulled low over his face.

The Grin Reaper!

Could it be Wiley? I feel strangely excited, but remind myself that he's no friend. I have a score to settle with the Reaper. No one tosses me to the ground and dumps my backpack in the garbage. *You're through, Reaper,* I vow. *I'm going to find out who you are and make sure everyone at school finds out too.*

This is a new twist to my finding skill, I observe with a wry grin.

Ducking behind cars, I move closer to the bus. At less than fifty feet away, there's no mistaking the furtive movements of the Reaper. He's creeping beside the tires, clearly intent on trouble. He lifts his hand and something silvery flashes. A knife? Is he going to slash the tires?

Sprinting forward a few cars, I duck behind a silver Prius, watching. The Reaper nears the door of the bus, his head tucked low. He stops, climbs up the steps, and reaches for the knob, but it doesn't open. He withdraws something the size of a pencil from his pocket. His back blocks my view, but when the door falls open, I know he's picked the lock. Wait till I tell Rune! Her hero is nothing more than a criminal.

He enters the bus, the steps folding up behind him.

What's he doing in there? Nothing good, that's for sure. I wait, not sure what to do. I could run get a teacher. But what if he leaves before I get back and I end up looking like a fool? Still, if I do nothing, he could trash Philippe's bus. And that's just wrong after Philippe generously donated his time to the school.

And why would the Reaper go after Philippe, anyway? Curiosity itches like a bad rash I shouldn't scratch. But I've never been good at doing what I'm supposed to, which is my only excuse for heading to the bus.

But as I get close, the door swings open. The automatic steps unfold again as if obeying the Grin Reaper's command. He hits the ground running, his feet flying.

Instinct takes over and I go after him. He heads back toward the school, turning down a path leading to classrooms. He pauses, glancing around, then disappears around a corner.

When I reach the walkway, he's gone. I keep running, straining my neck looking for him. As I near the cafeteria, I hear the hum of voices from the Singing Star rehearsal. The Reaper could easily slip inside and vanish into the chaos.

Increasing my pace, I reach the auditorium and grab for the door. But I hear a sound behind me. I whirl, and see dark clothes and a ski mask over dark eyes. He's leaning against the whitewashed wall, one gloved hand casually resting on the rough surface and the other tucked into his jacket pocket. I can't see his face, but I know he's grinning.

"What did you do?" I demand accusingly. I take a step forward, careful to keep an arm's distance between us. I doubt he's dangerous, but I don't trust him.

"Whatever do you mean?" he says in a mocking voice.

"You know exactly!" I'm furious he's not taking me seriously. "I saw you sneak inside Philippe's trailer."

"Delusional much?"

I glare. "You were carrying a knife when you went into the trailer but I didn't see anything in your hands when you came out. What have you done?"

"You thought that was a knife? It wasn't."

"I don't believe you."

"Have you always been such a skeptic?" he asks. "What do you think I did? Vandalized the big famous star's bus? Sorry, but you're wrong."

"I don't care what you did. But the principal will."

"I'm sure he will. Be a good little girl and go tattle to him."

"You want to get rid of me and it won't work."

"Your obsession with me is flattering, but you're not my type."

"Egotistical jerks aren't my type," I retort. And I can't believe I ever thought Wiley was hot (I'm ninety-five percent sure that's who this is). He's smug and too sure of himself. He's purposely baiting me because he wants me to leave so he can ditch his Reaper clothes and retreat back into obscurity.

"Shouldn't you report me?" he taunts. "What if I planted a bomb on his bus?"

"Did you?" I demand.

He shrugs. "Find out for yourself. Or wait around for the big kaboom. Hurry, time is running out."

I glare at him, then turn like I'm going to leave.

Mid-turn, I whirl back and lunge for him, hands reaching, grabbing the edge of his ski mask, pulling it off…

Revealing the Grin Reaper.

ELEVEN

Not Wiley, or even a Jay-Clone. It's the original.

"Jay Blankenship!" I shout.

I'm grinning as wide as his trademark smiley face. The infamous vigilante is the preppy, popular, egotistical son of the most respected judge in town. I love the irony! And I'm going to love exposing him.

His dark eyes, even when glaring, are softer now than when viewed through a slit in a ski mask. His blond lashes are long, curled, and almost girly, at odds with the hard lines of his cheekbones. When I've seen him around school, he always has an arrogant lift to his chin—he's handsome and he knows it. But up close, I can see the rough edges in his face and a small scar above his right eyebrow. *Not so perfect now*, I think.

"Give me my cap!"

"Of course," I say. With exaggerated politeness, I hold it out. His murderous glare doesn't scare me.

He snatches the mask roughly, then shoves it into his pants pocket.

"Aren't you going to put it back on to hide your identity?" I say, amused.

"There are other ways," he says mysteriously, peeling off his gloves and shoving them into his coat pocket.

Then he takes off the long coat and turns it inside out—revealing royal blue fabric hidden beneath the midnight black. He folds up the yards of excess fabric, transforming the concealing coat into his preppy letter jacket. He drapes it over his arm as if this is a new fashion style his Jay-clone followers will emulate. Whipping out a comb, he smooths back his blond hair, then parts it off-center, a wave falling across his forehead and softening the hard edges of his face. The Reaper is transformed back to the Prep.

I'm not sure who disgusts me more, the smug rich kid or the vandal. I touch a stained corner of my backpack—a reminder of his theft and brutal actions.

"You don't need to hide your identity anymore," I say coolly.

"Why not?" he demands.

"Figure it out."

"Are you threatening to expose me?"

I give a thin smile. "The word 'threat' implies that I might not go through with it. But I will."

He frowns. "You can't tell *anyone*."

"I'm going to tell *everyone*," I say, as if making a solemn promise.

"That would be a very bad idea."

"People will want to know the truth—especially your father."

His brows knit together, his faint scar stretching like a scowl. "Don't you understand that I'm helping people? Let's talk this over."

"I have nothing to talk about with you. But I have lots to tell the principal."

"Don't do that." He bites his lip. "Please."

"Why shouldn't I?"

"Because you're not the hard-hearted bitch that some people think you are."

"Sweet-talking me won't change my mind."

"Then I have no choice." His gaze shifts into a mask, something dangerous glittering behind his wry smile.

I continue to face him confidently. "You can't stop me from telling everyone," I say. "What a joke! The Grin Reaper is the son of the honorable Judge Blankenship. After my talk with the principal, I'll tell my friend Amerie. She loves dramatic news like this and will text it to the world."

He leans close to my face, his frown deepening like a dangerous line no one should cross. "You are *not* going to tell anyone."

"Oh?" I say, amused. "Why won't I?"

"Because everyone has secrets—including you."

"Yeah, right," I scoff.

"Find any dead bodies lately?" He leans close to ear and adds in an ominous whisper, "Beth Ann."

His hot breath burns my skin, his words a wildfire out of my control. "How—how did you…?"

"How did I find out your real name? And about your odd discovery in the hills?" He smiles wickedly. "I have my ways. Are you ready to negotiate now?"

His tone and expression are so cocky I want to slap him. But hearing my real name from his lips has stolen my voice. I simply nod.

"There's a storeroom around the corner. Come on." He glances up and down the path and over at the auditorium, then turns, gesturing me to follow.

I hesitate, not wanting to go anywhere with him. But he knows too much.

So I follow him to a door I've passed many times before but have never really noticed. He pulls a key ring from his pocket and tries a few keys until the door opens. I don't ask how he has keys to private school rooms. I have too many questions already.

He flips on a light as we enter. The room reeks of ammonia and lemon; metal shelves crammed full of cleaners and other materials line the walls. Brooms and mops lean in a corner like lazy sentries.

He turns toward me. I take a step back. We're so close in this small confined space that I can feel the heat of his energy. His smile is cool but his body is tense, a wild beast ready to pounce if I turn my back or show fear.

"How did you find out about me?" I fold my arms over my chest.

"My contacts keep me informed," he says mysteriously.

"Who are they?"

"No one at this school."

"Someone at the Sheriff's Department?" I guess.

"I never reveal my sources. You're still a minor, so your name won't be released to the public. All anyone knows is that a teenager found a grave of a baby."

I close my eyes, remembering the ragged blanket... the tiny fingers...

When I open my eyes, Jay a.k.a. Reaper is studying me.

"That must have been hard," he says quietly.

"As if you care?" I snap.

"So I'm not allowed to have feelings?"

"If you did, you wouldn't hurt people. You're all about revenge and punishment. Maybe some people deserve it, but who said you get to decide? Your father is a judge—not you."

His dark eyes narrow. "You don't know anything about my father."

"If he's anything like you, I don't want to!" I meet his angry gaze with one of my own. "Why are you going after Philippe anyway? He doesn't even go to this school."

"But he did."

"You can't possibly hold a grudge against him from back then."

"The grudge isn't for me. He stole something from a friend who trusted him."

"But it was at least two years ago. Isn't it kind of sick to hold onto a grudge like that? Philippe has reformed and made something of himself. All you've achieved is revenge, hiding behind a mask. When everyone finds out who you are, it'll be over."

"They won't know if you don't tell. This is my last year here, and when I leave, the Reaper goes too." He rakes his fingers through his blond hair. "I'm the only one at school who knows it was you who found the body. I've known since last night, but I kept it to myself. I wasn't going to tell anyone."

"How big of you," I say sarcastically.

"I'm a good guy even if you don't believe me."

"Good guys don't plant bombs."

"There isn't a bomb. I only said that to get rid of you. I'm for getting justice, not destroying stuff. All I left on the bus was a DVD. I promise it won't go boom—at least not in a physical way. I also promise to keep your secret."

"If I keep yours," I say angrily.

"A mutual agreement."

I clench my hands so I won't smack him with a broom or squirt lemon-scented air freshener into his eyes. I want to lash out because no one has ever made me feel so defeated.

He knows about me. I know about him. Damn.

"Okay." I hang my head. "You win."

"I always do," he says. "But to make this official, swear that you won't tell anyone who I am. I know you won't break a solemn swear."

"You mean because my mother is a minister?" I demand.

"No. She isn't you."

"Then how can you trust me?"

He tilts his head, studying me. "Even when you glare like that, your eyes give you away. You're trustworthy, honest, and loyal."

"A regular Girl Scout." I glance away because he's staring at me like my soul is naked. "But you're right—I won't go back on a promise. If you swear to keep my secret, I'll swear to keep yours."

"Fair enough. Shake on it." He holds out his gloved hand, waiting.

I'm reluctant to touch him, as if even a brief contact will somehow change me. But I'm no coward so I hold out my hand. He meets mine with a firm grip; I feel callused skin against my palm. I'm a little dizzy and blame it on the strong odors from the cleaning supplies. He holds on longer than necessary, but I remind myself why I hate him and that he's the total opposite of my type. Then he releases my hand, whirling for the door.

He leaves so fast that I blink and he's gone.

I look down, aware of something in my hand. Unclenching my fingers, I find a tiny yellow circle clinging to my skin.

A smiley face sticker.

———

I've made a pact with the devil.

This realization pounds in my head with each footstep as I walk home from school. I'm angry, but also feeling something close to excitement. It's not like I'm suddenly a fan of the Grin Reaper, but we've established an odd alliance... one of mutual mistrust and dislike.

When I pass The Hole Truth donut shop, I think guiltily of Rune. I've ditched her after school two days in a row.

It's taken a while to develop our friendship; we're both blunt, with an honesty that borders on rudeness, but these traits that might have pulled us apart have bound us closer together. I decide that I'll make things up to her tomorrow. She's going to be shocked when I tell her about Amerie and Philippe. Sneaking off together, holding hands, kissing!

Amerie takes everything so seriously that I worry she'll think Philippe's really interested in her, not just flirting. He's a pop star, after all, with lots of groupies chasing after him.

When I get home, I find K.C. tinkering in the garage. I'm relieved he's not working tonight. He says "okay" when I ask for a ride to Skarla's later. He even knows who she is, explaining that he has a few classes with her.

I avoid my parents by saying I have homework (true, but I'm not doing it yet) and retreating to my room. I pull out folders of music I've written, feeling critical of my songs. A few are okay, but I'm no professional and would die rather than show them to anyone. I don't really know why I write songs; it's a weird compulsion. A melody gets stuck in my head and the only way to let it go is to put it on paper. My latest song, untitled so I just call it "Pest," plays in my mind. I reach for my guitar.

Even after K.C. drops me off at Skarla's, "Pest" is still running through my head. I don't realize I'm humming it until Skarla invites me in and asks me the name of the song.

"It's nothing," I say.

"Really? Well it should be." Then she invites me to join the other girls in the family room.

Barbee and Micqui are wearing similarly styled dark

jeans and sweatshirts. Micqui calls out my name in a friendly welcome. Barbee merely shrugs; it's clear she doesn't want me here.

Skarla's in charge and gets straight to business. She hands me a sheet of music. I study the arrangement, noticing how the lyrics mostly repeat lame words like "Giddy-up!" and "Sweet, Sweet, Sweetheart" for a song called "Giddy-up Sweetheart." I strum a few notes on my guitar and feel like my ears are bleeding in protest.

Apparently I'm a minority of one, though, because the other girls love the song. When Skarla's parents come in with sodas and a tray of chips and cookies, they applaud enthusiastically. "Brava, brava!" says her father. And the way he's looking at her, supportive and proud, kills me. I can't remember my dad ever looking at me that way.

We go through the song about five hundred times, until it's running through my fingers and head. The words are sappy and the melody sucks, but a few note changes would help immensely. I consider suggesting this, but ultimately say nothing.

We take a break, and Skarla leans close to her friends, whispering. Immediately I'm on guard. Are they talking about me?

"I'll be right back," she announces loudly.

Micqui and Barbee share a look that shuts me out. I knew this would happen. You just can't trust people.

I set my face into a mask and mentally rehearse my reaction to being kicked out of the group. A shrug and smile to let them know I don't care. "I only did this as a favor for Amerie," I'll say.

Then Skarla comes back, her hands tucked behind her back. She tips her head to the side in a gesture that signals the other girls. They come beside her; unified against me. Why are they smiling?

"What's going on?" I ask cautiously.

"Surprise!" Skarla exclaims, reaching toward me with a bright pink hat in her hand. "A gift for you! You're one of us now."

They all look at me, waiting for my reaction.

I'm not a fan of western hats. And pink!? I don't think so.

But I'm relieved they didn't kick me out of the group— at least not until I find out who owns the locket. So I take the hat and even put it on my head. "Thanks," I say.

"You're welcome!" Skarla rushes to grab me in a warm hug. "I'll give you the rest of the costume as soon as I get it back from Priscilla. We're so glad to have you in our group. Thanks!"

"I haven't done much." I squirm out of her grasp.

"How can you say that?" Skarla is like a balloon of joy that's been popped on me. "After Priscilla quit, we didn't have a chance of winning. But you rescued us. And your playing is amazing. You're really talented."

I shrug, uncomfortable with praise.

When Skarla leaves the room, I turn to the Micqui and Barbee. "Is Skarla always so cheerful?"

"Always." Barbee takes a cookie from a tray on the coffee table.

"Skarla's cool," Micqui says. "She never even complains."

"Complains about what?" I ask, gesturing at the spacious, artfully decorated room. "She's popular, pretty, lives in a gorgeous house, and has supportive parents."

"Those aren't her parents," Micqui says. "Grandparents."

"So where are her parents?"

"Don't tell anyone at school," Barbee says in a hushed voice. "Her mother is in jail and her father died of an overdose."

I can't think of anything to say. I'm sobered and a little ashamed. Although I never said anything snarky, I'd mentally labeled Skarla as an over-bubbly fluff-brain. I judged her without looking any deeper, like most people do to me. I hate hypocrites—especially when I turn out to be one too.

As an unspoken apology, I'm nicer for the rest of practice. I don't even roll my eyes when I'm asked to hum the chorus of "Giddy-up Sweetheart."

When we finish, Skarla offers to drive me home. As I'm putting on my jacket, a button snags in my hair. I pull and tug until it loosens but it catches on the shoestring around my neck, sweeping the locket out from underneath my shirt. The plastic heart shines golden under the car's dome light.

"Pretty necklace." Skarla nods at the necklace as she starts up the engine.

"Pretty ugly is more like it."

"Depends on who gave it to you. Even tacky plastic is priceless if it's a gift of love," she replies philosophically. The car moves forward, the dome light softly fading until we're in near darkness. "Did your boyfriend give it to you?"

That question is wrong on so many levels that I almost laugh. "Not even close. This necklace isn't mine. I found it on a chair on the stage, on registration day for the contest."

"Meeting Philippe that day was sooooo amazing," she says, sighing. "Everyone gasped when he showed up in the auditorium. He signed autographs and posed for photos. Want to see one of us together? My skin still tingles where he put his arm around me. Then he led a Q and A session on the stage. Ohmygod. It was, like, amazing."

"You were on stage with him?" My brain clicks through events as she nods. "Then you must have seen whoever lost this."

She looks closer at the golden heart, then shakes her head. "Sorry. I've never seen it before."

"No one has," I say in frustration. "But I'm sure whoever lost it was on the stage with Philippe. I've been really obvious showing it around, but no one has claimed it and I can't think of any other way to find out."

"I can," Skarla says.

I raise my brows, surprised.

"Maybe I took a picture of it," she says. "I brought my camera that day, since I always post tons of pictures on my blog. I get hundreds of hits every day, which is so cool. I talk about where I went with my friends or what we're wearing or what we ate for lunch."

Exactly why I don't read blogs, I think. I gesture for her to go on.

"Since Philippe coming here is the most interesting thing to ever happen at Nevada Bluff High—he even brought his tour bus!—I wrote a really long post and uploaded all my photos. You know, when I was helping Amerie set up the chairs on the stage, girls were fighting over who got to sit next to Philippe. It's crazy the way girls freak out over him, but who can blame them?"

"Philippe is just another guy," I say, thinking of Amerie locking lips with him. She'll want to be his "one and only," not his "one of many." If I try to warn her, will she listen? Probably not.

"He's way more than that—he's perfect," Skarla says with a sigh. "I got great photos of him, and of everyone else on the stage, too."

"Everyone?" My hopes rise. At the very least, this will narrow my search.

"Yeah. Check it out."

Skarla hands me her cell phone.

TWELVE

I click through about a hundred photos. I don't see the locket, but I do find a clear shot of the people who went to the Q and A session. Seven fan girls and one guy sit in a circle of chairs surrounding Philippe and his manager. Amerie is so close to Philippe she's practically in his lap. I also recognize Barbee, Micqui, and Jessika from English Lit.

"Can you send me this picture?" I tap my finger on the camera.

"Sure." Skarla asks for my email. "I can include names, too, if you'd like."

"Thanks." I give her my email addy.

As we turn up the street to my house, excitement rushes through me like when I'm in finding mode and close to a solution. All I have to do is find out which of the girls sitting in that circle was pregnant last year, then confront her with the locket. She'll confess about the grave, and then my parents and Sheriff Hart will know I'm not involved.

When I get home, I'm lucky—no one is using the computer in the family room. It's a clunky older model, but it works most of the time. I'd rather have my own personal computer, of course, but that's not going to happen. My parents offered to buy me a laptop for my seventeenth birthday if I improved my GPA. I improved it, but by then Dad's job was history and so was my hope for a laptop.

I power up the clunk-puter and check my email for one from Skarla. I open the photo, comparing the faces to the names she included in her email. I enhance it to a larger size and study each person. Jessika and the guy, who's named Aidan, are both wearing necklaces—but not a gold heart hanging on a black shoelace.

I glance at each suspect, mentally crossing off Aidan, Philippe, and Philippe's manager Collette. I narrow my suspicions to the seven girls: Amerie DuPrau, Barbee Kingrey, Micqui Kingrey, Jessika Schillard, Ebony Mae Alexander, Veronique Samoun, and Ruby Rodriquez.

One of you lost the locket—and a baby, I think grimly.

But how do I find out which girl? I'll need more than suspicions and a photo to prove anything. I only know three of the girls: Barbee, Micqui, and Amerie. I start to cross off Amerie but then pause … what do I really know about her? She and Rune have been friends forever, which is how I got to know each her, but I'm not close with her like I am with Rune. I've been to Amerie's house a few times and met her stay-at-home mom, who sells Tupperware, and her kinder-garten teacher dad. She jokes that her parents are so normal, she must be a changeling switched at birth. I don't doubt it—there's more to her than wings and a sunny nature. Her rendezvous with Philippe proves that she can keep a secret.

If I still lived in Sheridan Valley, I'd ask Manny DeVries for investigative help. He's editor of the school newspaper and can find out anything. His brains are his best asset; his ego his worst. He's a brilliant computer geek, sexy in black dreds and he knows it. He's also a dating addict, going through girlfriends like it's a sport and he's aiming to medal. When I refused to date him we became friends instead, which is a better deal since he's unreliable as a boyfriend but amazingly loyal as a friend.

Why not ask him anyway? Being geographically apart doesn't end a friendship. So I shoot off a quick email—and get a reply within a minute:

> Send me the names and what you need to know.
> Will get on it ASAP.
> PS—How's it going in NV?

I reply:

> THX.
> Not great but not boring.

I forward the photo and the names and explain how I suspect one of the fan girls had a baby but hid the pregnancy. I added what the sheriff said about the bones being six to eight months old. I start to hit *send*, then think of someone else I'd like to know more about.

> PS. Need info on Jay Blankenship.

Then I hit *send* before I lose my nerve.

I play a computer game while I wait for his reply. As usual, Manny isn't just fast—he's accurate. He sends me pages of info including photos and school records (how does he get those?). I lean close to the computer screen, studying each photo. Most come from blogs and I jot down the dates they were taken, searching for a tell-tale baby bump. It's hard to tell, since most are face-shots. There's one of Micqui from last February and she looks heavier, but then another shot shows her skinny at a pool party over spring break. Barbee is at the same party, but all I can see is her face.

By the time I've gone through all of them, my eyes are blurry and I haven't found even have a hint of a baby bump.

While there are lots of photos of six of the girls, Manny forwarded none of Ruby Rodriquez. I only have Skarla's photo of her sitting on the stage with Philippe—she's thin, with black hair long enough to sit on. I search through school records (thanks Manny!) and check out her class schedule. She's a senior, and off-campus the second half of the day for a regional nursing program. There's no more information on her.

I have her schedule, though, so it'll be easy enough to find her at school on Monday. I may know more by then.

At least I have a place to start, which feels good.

There's a knock at my door and Amy shouts my name.

"Go away," I call out.

"Phone." Amy smacks the door.

I jump for the door, snatching the phone because I'm sure it's Manny with more information. I thank Amy then shut the door before she can ask noisy questions. I glance at Caller ID and only find "Unknown Caller" flashing on the display.

"Is this Thorn?" There's nothing familiar about the whispery girl's voice. All I can tell is that she's someplace with lots of background noise.

"Yeah," I answer cautiously. "Who's this?"

Another whisper. "You have my locket."

"Maybe I do." I don't want to scare her off. She has no way of knowing her locket led me to the grave. She only knows I found her locket. "But I can't just hand it over to anyone. Can you prove it's yours?"

"I saw you … wearing my gold … " I can't make out the rest of what she's saying over loud music and someone shouting in the background.

"Who are you?" I ask again.

"Bring it … to … " Background sound drowns out her words.

"Speak louder. I can't hear you."

"Meet me … Stardust … "

"Stardust Mall?" I guess. Amerie is always raving about the great discounts she finds at the mall and asking me to go with her. I always decline. Not a fan of malls.

"Yes," the caller says. "Tomorrow at noon."

"Why not wait till Monday at school?" I ask. This is a logical question, although I'm so curious to meet her that I'd find a way to get to the mall tonight if she asked.

"Can't wait," she admits, her voice strangely garbled. Is

she trying to disguise it? Does that mean I'd recognize her voice if she spoke normally?

"All right," I say as if this was a hard decision. "I'll meet you. Where at the mall?"

"The arcade."

"How will I know you?"

"I know you."

"That's not good enough. If I go out of my way to meet you at the mall, I deserve to know who I'm meeting."

"I'll explain when we meet."

Frustrated, I consider telling her I opened the locket, but that might scare her off. "Fine," I say. "I'll be there."

There's a long pause and if there wasn't so much noise around her, I'd think she hung up. But then she whispers, "Wear the locket."

The phone goes dead.

––––––––––

I oversleep, and when I wake up Mom has gone somewhere in her Jeep. Dad's car is in the driveway, but no way am I asking him for a ride. That leaves one person.

"K.C., can I borrow your car?" I ask when I find him tinkering on his vintage 1965 Ford Ranchero (he calls it a "classic"). He's been fixing it up since he bought it on Craigslist last month, but I have serious doubts that the clunker will ever leave our garage.

"Why?" He puts down a wrench and gives me a suspicious look.

"I just need it for a while. I won't be gone long. Please."

"Not without knowing what you're up to."

"Me?" I feign innocence. "I just want to go to the mall."

"You hate shopping."

"I'm meeting someone."

"A guy someone?" he teases.

"No. A girl."

K.C. pushes his hair from his face, leaving a grease streak across his forehead. "So why can't your friend pick you up?"

"She's not exactly a friend," I admit.

"So why meet her?" He rubs his chin, smearing more grease.

I hesitate. "It's the girl who lost the locket."

"Cool!" Excitement rises in his voice. "What are we waiting for? Let's go."

"Did I invite you?"

"I'm inviting myself. Any complaints?" He says it like he's joking, but I know his feelings will be hurt if I admit I don't want him to come along. Although he's a few months older than me, he acts more like a younger brother.

I grab a rag and toss it to him. "Wipe the grease off your face."

Grinning, he wipes his face, then takes his keys from his pocket and leads me over to his dented brown Toyota. He opens the door for me. Hinges creak loudly and the seats have rips covered with tape, but at least this car runs.

"So how'd you find her?" K.C. asks as we drive off.

"She called me—but she wouldn't tell me her name. She insisted on meeting at the mall."

"Strange. Why is this girl so secretive? If she wants her locket back, why not wait and get it at school? And why not tell you her name?"

I shrug. "I'll find out soon."

"You're not meeting a psycho chick alone. I'm sticking close to you."

The car jerks to a stop at a red light. "I don't need a bodyguard."

"Well, you got one."

He's trying to sound tough, which makes me smile because he's so not the bodyguard type. But he can be stubborn and there's no changing his mind.

Walking through the mall a short while later, I hear the electronic booms and blasts of the arcade before I see the flashing lights of the games.

"Don't follow me," I tell K.C.

"I'll be over there." He points to a NASCAR racing game and goes off to play.

I look around, fidgeting with the gold locket around my neck. There are more guys here than girls, so finding the caller shouldn't be too hard. I wander around, peering into faces and waiting for a look of recognition.

It's frustrating to meet someone I don't know. I'm not afraid—I mean, it's just a girl from school and I feel safe in a public place. She only wants her locket, which I can understand and even sympathize with, if her baby died naturally. But if the baby's death was deliberate, she deserves to rot in jail.

I walk through the arcade three times before I give

up. She's not coming. I was stupid to trust an anonymous voice on the phone. Angry at myself, I find K.C. in a crowd watching a kid slaughtering on House of the Dead. There's shouting and applause when he shoots zombies. I join him and watch too.

"He's almost beat the top score," K.C. yells in my ear, since that's the only way I can hear him.

I gesture that I want to leave.

"Just a minute," K.C. says, turning back to stare at the game.

The gamer kid is racking up his score when suddenly the screen goes black.

"What happened?" someone shouts.

"The game imploded!"

"Sabotage!"

But it's K.C. who moves over to the wall and lifts up a limp electrical cord. "The plug fell out," he says with a shrug, plugging it back in.

Instead of thanking him, the crowd turns on itself—arguing, shouting, and flinging accusations like pinballs gone wild.

I try to escape the mayhem but get a hard shove from behind. Someone pulls my hair and I cry out, stumbling sideways into a wall of bodies. It's all fast, and a blur of riotous gamers. Then there's a tug on my arm, and I look up to find K.C. pulling me out of the chaos. We push through bodies until we come out into the bright mall lights.

"What happened in there?" I bend over to catch my breath.

"That kid was just about to break the zombie-killing record. Probably whoever had the top score unplugged it. I can't believe how serious those guys get."

I point to his arm. "You're bleeding."

He touches a scratch on his neck and comes back with a blood-stained finger. "Those gamers are more dangerous than flesh-eating zombies," he jokes.

"Another reason to avoid malls," I say wryly. "Coming here was a waste of time."

"Psycho chick stood you up?"

"You may be right about her. Damn. I really expected to find out who owns the locket."

K.C. points at me with a curious expression. "I thought you were wearing it."

I reach up around my neck.

The locket is gone.

THIRTEEN

The anonymous caller tricked me!

She must have unplugged the zombie game, then snuck up behind me during the chaos, cut the shoelace, and stolen the locket. But why steal her own locket when I was going to give it to her anyway? Was it so I wouldn't see her face? Or maybe she'd lied about owning the locket and had planned to steal it all along. I knew it was risky to meet an unknown person but I did it anyway, letting her pick the place and obediently wearing the locket like she asked. And now I'd lost my only proof of another girl's guilt.

K.C. drives us back home, turning on the radio and purposely singing the wrong words in an off-key tone. I know he's trying to make me laugh, to distract me. But when one of Philippe's songs comes on, I turn the radio off.

My bad mood worsens when I enter the house and find Mom and some church ladies sitting around in the dining room, sipping tea and eating petite sandwiches. Why hadn't I remembered that Mom was having a tea social today?

Mouths pucker with disapproval at my army boots, barbed-wire belt, and black-streaked red wig. Mom stops talking with a chubby woman in a feathered yellow hat to turn toward me. I wait, hoping she'll offer me a cup of her delicious spiced-herbal tea. That's what she would have done at our old church, where the ladies had watched me grow up. But Mom blushes with embarrassment and gestures for me to leave.

I lift my chin like I don't care and stomp off in my army boots.

I go to the family room, hoping for an email from Manny. But my little brothers are blowing up alien dinosaurs and refuse to get off the computer. I ask nicely. I even say please. When that doesn't work, my short fuse explodes. I call them "spoiled greedy bloodsuckers," which makes Larry cry. Our arguing brings Dad in. He takes their side (of course) and orders me to my room to "contemplate my inconsiderate behavior."

I go to my room, but damned if I'm going to stay there like an obedient little girl. Climbing down my silk rope ladder, I sneak through the back yard. I consider hanging with K.C., but the smell of paint wafting from the garage means he's spray-painting his Ranchero. He's picked out a wicked shade of metallic ruby.

Aimless, I don't choose a destination. *Away from here*, that's where I want to go. Not only in miles but in time— back to Sheridan Valley where I felt in control of my life. I miss hanging out with Sabine, Manny, and my goth friends (there were more than two in the school!). I also miss the philosophical talks I used to have with Velvet, the owner of a cool New Age/candy shop. Velvet respected me like an adult, unlike my own parents.

Gray-black clouds boil over the western mountains and an acrid scent in the chilled air warns of rain. Brittle autumn leaves crunch under my boots as the wind shivers through my jacket, but I hardly notice the cold. I'm striding fast, heated by anger—not only at my brothers and my parents, but at myself for losing my temper. I have no idea where I'm headed until I turn onto Rune's street.

"About time you showed up," Rune says, her raven-black hair tucked under a scarlet scarf in a gypsy style, her face shades of crimson and lavender. A gathered skirt sways above red slippers as she shuts the door behind us.

"Did we have plans?" I raise my voice slightly to be heard over her wriggly pit bull, Casanova, who barks and wags a welcome.

"Not officially."

"So how did you know I'd come?" I bend down to scratch Nova behind his ears where he likes it, and he slobbers love all over my arm.

"It's Saturday."

She's right. Her home has become my weekend sanctuary.

"If you had a family like mine, you'd ditch home too." I follow her past the kitchen, dining room, and empty living room, Nova slurping at my heels.

"What's wrong with your family? I like them," Rune says.

"So take them—please. K.C. is the only one who doesn't drive me crazy."

"But he's not actually a blood relative."

"My point exactly." I blow out a long-suffering sigh.

I follow Rune into her bedroom. Casanova chases behind us, then jumps up on pillows in the window seat, curling into a ball like he's part cat.

We don't shut the door because there's no one else around. Rune's an only child, with ultra-busy Realtor parents who spend more time showing other peoples' homes than living in their own. In the couple of months I've known Rune, I've only seen her parents once.

Rune doesn't turn on the ceiling light; instead she lights incense candles that flicker shadows onto her lavender walls. "Admit it, Thorn," she says, settling down on a plush blue pillow. "You came over because you can't resist my twisted humor."

"You're twisted all right—in a good way." I inhale a faint scent of sandalwood, already starting to relax. "Is that a new shade of lip gloss?"

"Romany Rose. You can borrow it." She opens her Celtic Knot rectangular wooden makeup box and sorts through tubes until she finds the right one. "We can try out different face-painting styles from my *Goth Craft* book."

"Sure, why not?" I shrug. "Wanna invite Amerie to join us?"

"If we don't, we'll never hear the end of it. You know how she hates missing out and assumes we'll talk behind her back."

"We might," I say with a secret smile, thinking of what I know about Amerie and wondering if Rune knows, too. If not, should I tell her?

Rune hands me *Goth Craft* and I flip through it as I make myself comfy on a satin pillow. We never sit on her bed or in chairs, preferring the oversized pillows piled on the floor. Her room is decorated in a mix of goth and Arabian—moon signs painted on the ceiling, gauzy black curtains, and colored beads strung across her closet instead of a door.

"I'll text Amerie." Rune reaches for her phone. "I tried last night but she hasn't replied. She's been super busy since the contest."

"Not only the contest." I press my lips together.

"Oh?" Rune scoots her pillow closer to mine. "What do you know that I don't?"

"News more shocking than a museum of cockroaches."

"What? Tell me!"

"Yesterday I saw her in the school parking lot with—" I pause. "A guy."

"A boyfriend! I knew it!" Rune's dark eyes shine. "I caught her texting all secret-like, then she hid her phone when she noticed me watching. I asked who she was texting and she said it was just contest stuff, but it was obvious she was lying—and I know why."

"You do?" I arch a brow.

"She's going out with a contestant, which is probably against the rules, or maybe she's ashamed to tell us because the guy is a freshman. My theory is that it's Aidan Morgan." Rune snaps her fingers like she's smarter than Sherlock Holmes and Einstein cloned together.

"Amerie is definitely *not* into Aidan," I say with a firm head shake. Aidan's tall and awkward. His singing voice is good, but when he opens his mouth he makes weird expressions like a bird bobbing for worms.

Rune crosses her arms over her chest. "Why else would she keep it a secret?"

"Contestants aren't the only ones involved with the contest," I point out.

"What do you mean?"

I hesitate. "I shouldn't tell you, since Amerie is my friend too, and if she doesn't want anyone to know, I should respect that."

"Tell me or I'll smack you with a pillow." Rune raises a wicked beaded pillow.

"Put down your weapon." I throw up my hands in mock surrender. "But you can't repeat this to anyone."

"As if I would!" she says indignantly. "Is the guy a volunteer like Amerie?"

I shake my head.

"A singer or musician?"

"Both."

"Is he any good?"

"Really good." I hide a smile. Rune isn't the only one who can dish out dramatic suspense. "Philippe."

"No freaking way!"

"It's true." I cross my heart with fervor. "I saw them coming out of his tour bus."

"That doesn't mean anything. She's working on the contest."

"They were kissing."

Rune's mouth falls open, candlelight glinting golden off

her tongue stud. "What were they doing on his bus? Do you think...?"

"I hope not. He's not her type. Amerie's too trusting and he's too experienced."

"For sure. Philippe's dating drama is infamous. He's always with a new girl." Rune purses her black-lined red lips. "Don't get me wrong, he's hot and I'd jump his bones if he rattled them my direction. But I wouldn't take a player like him seriously. Not Amerie, though. She'll fall hard. She'll expect a formal engagement, marriage, kids, and to settle down in a Hollywood mansion. This is so not good."

"I completely agree," I say, frowning.

"So it's up to us to stop this."

I give Rune an *are you crazy* look.

But I know that she is crazy, and stubborn too. She's determined to rescue Amerie by breaking up her romance. I'm skeptical, but talking about Amerie's problems does distract me from my own ... for now. So we spend the next few hours coming up with wild ideas that won't work (kidnapping Amerie) and a few ideas that might (showing Amerie magazine photos of Philippe with other girls).

Before I leave, I check my email on Rune's computer. Manny has sent me some more photos, including a photo of Ruby taken at a school pep rally last April. I hardly recognize her—she has a double chin, round face, and chubby figure, drastically different from how she appears in the photo Skarla took a few days ago.

I think that Ruby is the guilty one.

When I get home, I open my email and study the photos again. Based on the apparent pregnancy timeline and the other photos I've seen, I can eliminate all of the suspects now except for Ruby and striking, dark-skinned Jessika. I don't know Jessika, since she's a sophomore and we don't share any classes, but in the photos she's always dressed in stylish layers that could hide a possible baby bump. I circle her name as a "maybe," but Ruby is now Suspect #1.

Sunday afternoon, I rehearse with the CCCs at Skarla's house. When we break for lunch, I steer the conversation to our competition and subtly ask about Ruby and Jessika. The CCCs don't know Ruby, but Micqui and Barbee live next to Jessika. Micqui confides that Jessika is into girls, not guys. I cross Jessika off my list.

While I'm washing dinner dishes, staring at my own reflection in a darkened window, I think about Ruby. She must have found out she was pregnant not long before school started last year, then faced months of fear and hiding until denial turned into tragedy. That would explain her transformation. Not only her drastic weight loss since last spring, but why she'd switched to snug, sexy clothes.

But how can I convince Ruby to confess? Stealing the locket back shows she'll go to drastic measure to hide her secret—she'll never confess unless I can show her undeniable proof or trick her. And I need to do it soon. If I don't prove my innocence before the news leaks that I'm the girl who found the grave, there will be rumors blaming me and Mom could lose her job.

Monday morning I'm not only ready for school early, I'm ready with a plan. A simple deception. I'll confront

Ruby with a handful of dark hair snipped from one of my wigs. I'll say I cut the hairs from the curl in the locket, and I'll threaten to turn it over to the sheriff if she doesn't admit the truth. She'll be too shocked to come up with a lie. I'll borrow the electronic voice recorder Mom uses to practice her sermons and record Ruby's confession, then play it back later for the sheriff.

"Why up so early?" K.C. asks when I come downstairs for breakfast and find him eating alone.

"Um ... I need to talk with someone before class."

"I'm leaving early for a make-up quiz. Want a ride?"

"That would be great," I tell him. I turn to grab a cereal bowl but notice he's just standing there, almost bursting with an odd grin. "Why do I get the feeling there's something you're dying to tell me?"

"Because you're psychic."

"Not me. That would be Sabine."

"If you say so." But he gives me a knowing look.

"So what's up?" I ask.

"I finally finished!" he announces, as if proclaiming he's solved world problems like starvation and global warming. Despite usually being so quiet and ordinary that he blends in with the ozone, K.C. is extraordinary when his eyes shine like this and energy sizzles in his attitude.

And just like that, I know what's he's going to say. I'm not psychic; I simply know his deepest passion.

"The Ranchero is done!" I exclaim.

He nods proudly. "After two months, it's ready to roll.

And I'm inviting you to be my first passenger. Want to ride to school in style on my inaugural ride?"

A 1965 Ranchero won't impress our classmates, especially cowboys with jacked-up pickup trucks, but K.C. has at least one fan: me. His car shines with its new metallic red paint, the dents are pounded out, and there are sleek silver hubcaps and an eagle hood ornament with wings spread ready for flight. The engine roars to life at a twist of a key. It's hard to believe this junker he bought for fifty bucks runs like new, but K.C. pampers it like a million-dollar baby.

When we get to school, he parks it at the edge of the parking lot away from other cars. He pats the winged hood eagle, then strides off with a new sense of pride.

I pull my folder out of my backpack to check Ruby's schedule, then determinedly head to her first class. I try not to prejudge her, even though I know it'll be hard to feel sorry for her if she cold-bloodedly killed her own baby. It's more likely the baby died naturally, and she was alone and panicked.

I go into the classroom and find Ruby, who's looking even thinner than she did in the photo taken on stage with Philippe. *Too thin*, I think, frowning. She's wearing a silk sea-green top, a sea-blue mini-skirt, and knee-high suede boots. When I call her name she looks me up and down, brows raised. "What do you want?"

"To talk."

"Why? I don't know you." Her tone is more curious than rude. "Although I've noticed you—you're the new goth girl. Isn't it painful to wear a barbed wire belt?"

"The barbed wire looks sharp but it's not. I'm Thorn."

"Weird name. Is it real?"

"Real enough." I'm not good at casual chit-chat, so I hold up the folder and pull out the photo of her where she's almost twice the size she is now. "This is you, isn't it?"

"Not any more, thank God." She grins. "Can you believe how fat I was?"

"I wasn't going to ... um ... say fat."

"Go ahead, say it. Fat, fat, fat. I've slammed the door on that phase of my life. It seems like years ago."

"Not that long." I know the date by memory. "Only last April."

"Well, it seems like a lifetime. But why do you have a photo of me?"

"I know how you lost the weight," I say, in a solemn way like I'm proclaiming the end of the world. Her world, anyway.

"Who doesn't?" Ruby rolls her eyes. "Not a big secret. I mean, I lost sixty-five pounds."

"I'm more interested in how you gained it," I say, then gesture around the room. "Let's move away from everyone else. You don't want others to hear this."

"Why not? I'm proud of my weight loss," she says with a sway of her slim hips. "I worked my butt off—literally—to drop three dress sizes. I worked out three hours a day, cut back on carbs, and gave up soft drinks."

"You gave up much more," I say sadly. "Stop lying."

Her expression goes from friendly to hostile. "What are you talking about?"

I meet her gaze. "I just want to know the truth."

She lowers her voice so only I can hear. "You can't prove anything. Besides, it's my business. Not yours or anyone else."

"Are you sure about that?"

Her lower lip trembles. "Why do you care? You don't know anything about me."

"I know that lies hurt people. How did you really lose the weight?"

"As if I'd tell you something I haven't even told my best friend!"

I shake my head at her. "You've lied to your best friend?"

"I couldn't tell her ... but if she finds out, she'll hate me."

"Not if she's a real friend," I say gently. "Be honest or you'll regret it forever."

I stare her down, unblinking, determined to break her—and it works.

Her slim shoulders sag. "I—I've wanted to tell Gabrielle, but she wouldn't understand. And it's been cool how everyone says I look way better. Gabrielle thinks it was from exercise and dieting ... but it wasn't. I—I lied to my own best friend. I'm the worst person in the whole world."

"Not the worse," I say, in a suddenly generous mood. This is going much easier than I expected. "Everything will be all right if you're honest."

"I have no idea how you found out or why you even care, but it's a relief that someone knows," Ruby said, sighing. "Lying to Gabrielle sucks. I die whenever she compliments my new figure. She's going to hate me when she finds out."

"Admitting what really happened is the only way to get on with your life. Be honest with everyone—including the sheriff."

"Sheriff?" Her eyes widen.

I nod solemnly. "He needs to know the truth."

"You're flipping crazy!" She steps away from me, shaking her head. "I didn't break any laws. My mother signed the papers and took me to the clinic. Lying about having stomach surgery wasn't honest, but it was totally legal."

"You had stomach surgery?" I stare at her, startled.

"Well, duh. Isn't that what we've been talking about?" She gives me a curious look. "I mean, get real! Sixty-five pounds in six months? How else could I lose that much weight so fast?"

FOURTEEN

Minutes later I'm in homeroom, pretending to work on a history assignment but actually sneak-reading my notes. No matter how many times I calculate the dates and names, I come to the same conclusion.

Ruby has to be guilty.

Only she isn't...

How could I make such an epic mistake? I go through the list again, but the dates don't fit any of the other girls—they were all too thin last spring. Yet someone is guilty. It's no accident that the day after I flaunt the locket, it gets stolen. The hidden curl is more than a memento; it's evidence.

So which girl is guilty?

I read through the list again, swearing, crossing each name off until there's no one left. But how is this possible? And I have a feeling, like an itch I can't reach, that I'm missing an important clue...

The first batch of Singing Star auditions are today, and Amerie is a blur rushing through halls. While she doesn't have time for friends, I'm sure she's making time for Philippe. I'm relieved we don't have to audition until tomorrow. If we make it, we'll perform in the finals on Friday.

Word must have leaked that the "freaky goth" is now a Cotton Candy Cowgirl. Kids and teachers stop me in the halls to wish me luck in the contest. When I see Ruby studying in the library with a chubby blond girl wearing pink braces, she tilts her head toward her friend (Gabrielle, I assume) and gives me a thumbs-up. My comforting status of "outsider" has shifted to "involved."

But the weirdest moment occurs between classes. When I'm crossing the quad, I pass five guys in blue letter jackets. Wiley doesn't even notice me, or maybe he's forgotten we met in detention. But Jay's dark eyes find me. He offers me a gloating smile and a sly wink. Then he swaggers down the walkway with his friends.

I'm sweating, even though the weather is close to freezing and I'm bundled in layers. My emotions tumble in a landslide of confliction. I'm intrigued, disgusted, insulted, and yet oddly excited. Jay is so arrogant, assuming I'm no threat to him. But no one controls me.

The Grin Reaper better watch out.

When the bell rings for lunch, I hurry to meet Rune. But I don't make it far before I hear my name. I look up just as a rush of pink enthusiasm shoves papers into my hand.

"I've rewritten the lyrics," Skarla announces proudly. She's wearing her CCC outfit even though our group isn't scheduled to audition today.

"No way!" I object. "We'll only have a day to practice this."

"A day is enough. I changed the first and last stanzas so they make more sense."

"We can't change everything at the last minute," I tell her.

"A lot can get done in a day." Skarla's smile never falters as she points to the paper in my hand. "Don't you love these new lyrics?"

I skim the sheet music, groaning because if our song was sappy before, now it's sappy enough to be bottled and poured over pancakes. I tell Skarla I prefer the old version, but she waves away my objections and insists on a group vote right now.

"Can't," I say. "I'm meeting a friend for lunch."

"This won't take long," she insists.

"Five minutes," I concede, then I reluctantly follow her into the cafeteria.

We join Micqui and Barbee at a back table and immediately get into a heated argument about whether the word "heart" can be rhymed with "breath." *No*, the answer is *no*. But does anyone listen to me? Nope.

By the time I escape to finally join Rune, I can't find her. *Just great*, I think in frustration. Rune will be mad I stood her up. She has a short fuse and can hold grudges forever. I want to explain, but she isn't by her locker. It's better to let her cool down, anyway. After watching the auditions, I'll find Rune and sweeten my apology with donuts.

The auditions are held after school so that everyone can come and cheer on the contestants. When I enter the auditorium, the vast room is packed and echoing with noisy voices. I'm straining my neck looking for the CCCs when they find me.

"Wait till you hear our brilliant new idea!" Skarla's wearing her pink hat and the brim bounces over her shining eyes.

"What?" I brace myself, still annoyed by her last "brilliant" idea.

She glances around, then tucks her head to whisper, "Too crowded here. Someone might overhear and steal our idea. I'll explain everything at my house."

"I thought we weren't meeting until seven?" I frown.

"Change of plans. We have so much to do we're practicing right after auditions. My grandparents are making dinner. I assume you like Italian. We have to whip our act into shape, which means working extra hours to win."

Not so interested in winning, I think. More interested in repairing any damage to my friendship with Rune. But I give up and agree to come.

"I'll give you a ride, and we can stop by your house to pick up your guitar," Skarla says.

"I brought my guitar along. It's in a friend's car."

"Good thinking." Skarla nods in approval. "I hope you're a quick learner, because I've come up with a fantabulous idea. We'll dazzle the judges by doing more than singing."

"What?" I ask suspiciously.

Skarla folds her arms to her chest and kicks up her feet. "Clogging."

I stare at her like she's talking in a strange language.

"Haven't you heard of clogging?" Skarla asks. "It's like

tap dancing, country-style. Barbee performs at festivals with a clogging group and she taught me. It's easy-peasy! You'll pick up the steps quick like I did."

"Not going to happen." I purse my lips together.

"Why not?" Skarla's hands fly to her cheeks.

"I signed on to play the guitar. Period."

"But playing the guitar while you clog will wow the judges."

I want to "wow" her—right in her mouth with my fist. That would be the quickest way to end this torture. And why am I even standing here? I only joined the CCCs to find out which contestant owned the locket. But I haven't been accused, or arrested for a crime, and only one person at school knows I found the grave. And now I don't even have the locket anymore.

So I tell them I quit.

"I knew you'd bail on us," Barbee says angrily.

Micqui gently touches my arm. "Please reconsider. Your playing makes everything sound so good. We need you. you," she begs. "Please don't go."

"You need someone who can play guitar and dance too," I say. "That's not me."

"You're better than Priscilla," Micqui says. She looks over to Skarla for help. "Tell her she can't go. You told me yesterday how impressed you were with her playing and that her talent could help us win."

Skarla nods. "It's true. You're an amazing musician, Thorn. With you playing for us, our chances of winning are huge. I'll do whatever it takes to win." The desperation in

Skarla's voice surprises me; it's like winning the competition is life-and-death important to her.

Something clicks in my head.

I visualize the photograph of the seven fan girls sitting on stage around Philippe. I started off with those seven suspects: Barbee, Micqui, Jessika, Amerie, Ebony Mae, Veronique, and Ruby. Each one has been crossed off my list. No one is left.

But I overlooked someone. How could I miss something so obvious?

There was another girl on stage with Philippe that day, but she wasn't in the photo—she was behind the camera.

I study Skarla in a new way. She's friendly, but she's guarded when it comes to her personal life. I wouldn't even know that she had a bitter breakup with her boyfriend last year or that her mom's in prison and her father is dead if Barbee and Micqui hadn't told me. Skarla is much deeper and more secretive than people know, I now realize. Her cheerful smile is a mask hiding her pain, like the Grin Reaper's ski mask hides his identity.

"I'll stay," I announce abruptly, without actually thinking it through. I just know I need to find out more about Skarla.

"Great! Unlike some people who have no faith, I knew you wouldn't really quit." Skarla glances triumphantly at Barbee, who turns away with a scowl.

"But I absolutely positively refuse to dance," I add firmly.

"As long as you play your guitar, we'll do the clogging."

Would she look so relieved if she knew I was only staying in the group to spy on her? If she's hiding the golden locket and a tragic baby secret, I'll find out.

Skarla, Barbee, and Micqui take seats close to the stage, but I stay in the back, away from the noisy hustle. Collette, wearing her usual red suit, comes to the podium.

"Welcome to the first round of auditions for the Singing Star contest," the manager announces. "Philippe and I are honored to be here among all you fine young people."

She's not *that* much older than us, I observe wryly. Maybe ten years, tops.

"As you all know, this fine school is Philippe's alma mater." She sweeps her hand to gesture at Philippe, who flashes his mega-watt smile. The audience screams and shouts "Philippe!" so loudly I have to cover my ears.

Collette waves her hands for silence, then wishes all the contestants good luck.

Overhead lights flash, then dim, and the first entrant goes on—a girl with long black braids that she twirls nervously as she squeaks out a Mariah Carey song. And I do mean "squeaks." The audience groans and there's silence instead of applause. The girl runs offstage in tears.

The second performer, Veronique, plays a mean keyboard while she sings. The audience and judges obviously love her. I notice fairy wings at a corner of the stage near the judges; Amerie sits two chairs away from Philippe. She applauds, but her gaze shift over to Philippe, luminous and adoring. She's totally into him ... does he feel the same way?

Next up is Jessika, who sings a duet with a perky

red-haired girl all dressed in green like a leprechaun. They harmonize well and I'm sure they'll make the finals.

Several more solo singers go on and only one of them is any good—Ruby. But the song she picked is for a soprano; it's totally wrong for her, and she's off-key. It'll be a crime if she doesn't make the finals because of poor song choice. After finishing she runs offstage, her face red with shame. When I realize she'll come past me, I stand up and step into the aisle, blocking her.

"Wait, Ruby." I gently take her arm.

She stares at me with astonishment. "You again."

"Yeah." I smile wryly. "Just saying good luck."

"Don't bother. I totally blew it." Her face reddens and her eyes glint like she's close to crying. "Missed the high note completely. I'm such a loser."

"No, you're not." I walk with her out of the auditorium. "You were one of the best. I think you'd do better with the right song."

Sniffling, she shakes her head. "You keep showing up and doing things that help me. What are you? My fairy god-mother? Are you going to give me the perfect song with a twist of your magic wand?"

"Sorry, no wand." I shrug. "But I can suggest some songs."

"What's the use? I'll never make the finals."

"You don't know that. If you do make it, switch things up. Sing something deep and soulful."

"I hate depressing songs. Upbeat songs are more fun."

"Listen to them, then, but don't sing them. You need a bluesy song to really belt out and show your range."

"Like what?"

I try to think of songs, but nothing fits. Then my own melody, "Pest," jumps into my head, refusing to leave. Ironically, it would be a great match for Ruby, except for small details like there are no lyrics and I never share my songs. But Ruby is looking at me so miserably, and I feel guilty for grilling her earlier, accusing of something far worse than she knows. So I start humming "Pest."

When I finish, she flashes a smile that lights up her face like a spotlight shining on a diva. "Oh. My. God. That's so ... so amazing. Where can I download it?"

"You can't."

"Why not?"

"It's not a real song ... I mean ... " I suck in a deep breath and blow it out. "Okay, if you must know—and don't repeat this or I'll have to kill you—I wrote it. But I can't tell you the lyrics because there aren't any."

"Oh ... wow. I'm impressed."

"Don't be. I can't even write words for my own songs."

"Lyrics aren't hard, but creating a song like that is brilliant."

"It's nothing." I glance down at my army boots.

"Can I hear it again?"

"Well ... okay."

I hum my song a few more times until the final bell rings and kids pour out from the auditorium. I wish Ruby good luck again and hurry toward the parking lot to get my guitar.

The main walkway is crowded so I cut down another path. I take the long route, behind the cafeteria—and glimpse a long black jacket and dark ski mask up ahead. My breath catches. There's no mistaking the yellow smile on the Grin Reaper's ski mask.

I start after him, my backpack jostling against my shoulders. I have a good idea what Jay's up to.

He turns left toward the staff parking lot, where Philippe's bus is parked. I was right—he's still out to get revenge on Philippe.

I reach open pavement and see the gleaming tour bus. But I don't see the Reaper. Could he already be on the bus? But there hasn't been enough time for him to pick the lock again. Where did he go? I scan the lot for hiding places. I remember him saying that last time, he left an "explosive" DVD for Philippe. What does that mean?

I wait forever—or about five minutes, according to my watch.

But there's no sign of Jay.

Shrugging, I give up and head toward the student parking lot to meet K.C.

As I approach, I hear shouts and notice a crowd gathering. I wonder if there's a fight. I don't want to get near that kind of drama, but I have to go that way to get to K.C.'s car. As I'm wondering how long I'll have to wait for K.C. to show up and unlock the doors, I see that he's already there. His back is turned to me, but I know immediately that something is wrong.

Then I see his beautiful rebuilt Ranchero, slashed with ugly smears of paint.

Dark bloody letters drip crude ugly words.

Spelling hate.

FIFTEEN

I run to K.C., who is staring at his car in shock, and put my arm around him. His face is pale as a corpse, as if he's dead inside. He gently traces his finger along the broken wing of the hood eagle. "She'll never fly again."

"The wing can be fixed," I assure him. "And so can the car."

Around me I hear murmurs, mostly of sympathy, but one guy laughs and I turn around furiously, ready to rip out his tongue and twist it around his neck. When I see his blue letter jacket, I think it's Jay—until he lifts an arm and I see a rattlesnake tattoo. Wiley nudges his buddy and laughs again.

Furious, I start to go after him, but K.C. jerks me back. I hear Wiley laugh again and murmur two words that rock me with outrage: *Grin Reaper*.

Did Jay do this? Is there a smiley sticker stuck somewhere on K.C.'s car? Now I'm so mad that I really might rip out Wiley's tongue. I want him to suffer a horrible death—and Jay, too.

I'll get revenge on the king of getting revenge. I suspected Jay was up to trouble when I saw him sneaking around, but I thought his target was Philippe.

Why go after K.C., who is kind and gentle and never would hurt anyone? Unless this isn't about K.C. Could the vandalism be a warning from the Reaper? *Keep my secret or next time will be worse.*

There is no worse, though, I realize as I look at K.C.'s stricken face. Hurting the Ranchero was cruel. The car can be repaired, but the pride and joy K.C. felt this morning has been destroyed.

When a teacher shows up and orders the crowd to clear out, I stay with K.C., still holding his hand for support. Someone must have called 911, too, because police lights swirl red and blue.

Sheriff Hart doesn't react when he sees me. He's all business, working with his deputy to ask questions, take photos, and write up a report. I'm wondering why the sheriff came in person for a minor crime (minor to them, anyway). I find out when he pulls me aside.

"A moment of your time, Miss Matthews," he says politely, shutting his notebook and tucking it into his pocket.

"Uh … sure."

"Is that young man your beau?" he asks with a glance over at K.C., who is still giving a statement to the deputy.

"He's just a good friend."

"But he lives with you?"

"He's staying with my family." I explain how K.C. was living on the streets until we took him in.

"How convenient for you," he says, with a sly arch of his brows. He can't possibly think that K.C. and I had anything to do with the grave. But I can tell by his expression that this is exactly what he's thinking.

"K.C. is like another brother to me," I insist. "We have never been ... like that."

"Duly noted." His tone is professional but it's obvious he doesn't believe me.

"If you think I had anything to do with the ... the grave, you're wrong. I've only lived here a few months, and you said the ... um ... bones had been there six to eight months."

"That was only a calculated guess. I never assume anything until I have all the facts."

"What about the DNA results?" I ask.

He shakes his head. "Unlike what you see on TV shows, lab results can take weeks, even months."

"So until then I'm your only suspect?"

"Actually, I don't suspect you."

I stare at him, surprised. "Then why are you still questioning me?"

He purses his lips, regarding me thoughtfully. "Your version of events doesn't add up with the facts. I am not a believer in coincidence. It's unlikely you randomly drove to the remote spot and just happened to dig up a grave."

"I didn't dig it up!" I say indignantly. "A wild animal must have done that."

"But a wild animal didn't bury that body, and I think you know who did. Why else would you drive to the exact spot? Someone must have told you how to find that grave."

"No one told me anything."

"I admire loyalty among friends, but your friend isn't being fair to you." He leans closer. "If you tell me who she is, I can help. It'll be easier on you both and save everyone time. Lots of girls get in trouble, then panic and do things they regret later, but as long as they're truthful, they can usually avoid a prison sentence."

Prison! I think of Skarla, who has been so cool to me. She's trying to make something of herself despite a dead father and a mother in jail. If I tell the sheriff what I suspect, Skarla could end up in prison, too.

I fold my arms across my chest. "That's all I have to say."

"We'll talk again soon," he says politely, but it feels like a threat. Then he joins his deputy.

From behind me, a familiar voice asks, "Why was the sheriff talking to you?"

I turn to find Skarla. She shifts her feet nervously and is jerky like she's hopped up on energy drinks ... or scared.

"He was asking about K.C. because of what happened to his car." I point to the Ranchero.

"I didn't realize that guy was your friend," Skarla says with a sympathetic glance at K.C., who is now being questioned by Sheriff Hart. "I don't remember seeing him around."

"K.C. gets that a lot. He's one of those average guys no one notices."

"He's getting noticed now—but not in a good way." Skarla frowns. "That's horrible about his car. The tagger can't even spell. They forgot the 'c.'"

I ball my fists. "Of course the idiot, ignorant, stupid-ass tagger can't spell. If I find who did this, I'll kill him."

"You don't mean that." She puts a hand on my shoulder. "There's nothing else you can do here. Sorry about your friend's car, but I'm guessing this means you need a ride to my house." She hooks her arm through mine. "Come on."

I don't want to leave K.C., but when he tells me his auto shop boss is coming to tow the Ranchero to his shop and fix it free of charge, I grab my guitar.

On the drive to Skarla's house, I borrow her cell to call home. Mom is overjoyed, as usual, when she finds out who I'm with. Apparently Skarla's grandparents attend Mom's church and are "delightful people." Mom doesn't even give me a curfew. I try Rune's cell, but she's not taking my calls.

Barbee and Micqui are already waiting at Skarla's and we get right to work. Fortunately I don't have to sing the sappy new lyrics. I don't have to participate in the clogging lesson, either. Barbee is really good, but Micqui nearly trips over her feet. When Micqui accidentally kicks Barbee, I cover my mouth to hide my laughter.

After an hour of kicks and swearing, the clogging routine fits smoothly into our act. We open with strums of my guitar, then sing a few stanzas and finish with the clogging. I have to give Skarla credit because she's right—singing *and* dancing could push the Cotton Candy Cowgirls into first place.

When Skarla's grandparents announce dinner is ready, I set down my guitar and follow everyone into the dining room. The scent of tomato, cheese, spices, and sourdough bread makes my stomach growl. The lasagna looks home-made and delicious, but it will have to wait—this is my only chance to find out Skarla's secrets.

After taking a few bites of Caesar salad, I excuse myself to go to the bathroom. But I pass the bathroom and sneak into Skarla's bedroom.

The few times I've been in it before were quick, and while I'd glanced at some photos on a cork board, I hadn't seen any clues about a hidden pregnancy. I don't have much time now, either, so I close my eyes and search inside myself for my finding radar. I'm tempted to open my eyes, but something tells me I'll see more with my sixth sense.

So I move slowly, arms stretched and senses heightened. I touch a bed post, chair back, desk top, computer, door ... and nothing unusual happens. I'm close to the window now, feeling the brush of curtains on my arm. My pulse quickens and I have a strong impulse to reach down. When I do, my fingers meet smooth curved wood and shivers tingle through me.

I open my eyes and stare down at a carved wooden trunk half-hidden underneath a quilt. I'm breathless like I've been running. *Not much time*, I think urgently, and worry the trunk will be locked. But the curved lid lifts easily.

What I see inside makes me gasp.

A neatly folded pile of clothes.

Tiny baby clothes.

———

I can hardly think about anything else during the rest of

rehearsal. I stare at Skarla so intently that she asks if I'm okay. *No*, I think, *and neither are you.* But I say everything is fine, because it would be cruel to blurt out my suspicions in front of the other girls. Besides, what if I'm wrong? (Again!) I don't want to make the same mistake I did with Ruby. Next time I accuse someone, I need to be one hundred percent positive, which means checking facts with Manny.

We practice so long that it's dark when I finally get home. The house is strangely quiet except for a rumble of the television from my parents' room. I head for the family room, glad my siblings are in bed so there's no battling over the computer. There's an email with an attachment from Manny. The attachment is labeled *Justice Blankenship*, which puzzles me at first because I asked for information on Jay, not his father. But when I read further, I find out Jay's full name is Justice Hamilton Alexander Blankenship the Third. No wonder he prefers a nickname.

I skim through the file, noting Jay's academic excellence, community service, and celebrated sport achievements. Blah, blah, boring. A few photos highlight his winning moments in soccer, wrestling, and track; he's always grinning in that smug way that's as fake as the grin on the smiley sticker. Yet I notice something deeper in one photo—a tightening of his jaw and a grin that doesn't reach his dark eyes.

If you're the one who vandalized K.C.'s car, I tell his photo, *I will make sure you suffer in unimaginable, horrible ways.*

Frowning, I close the file and return to my email.

I send a message to Manny, asking for information on Skarla and tell him about the baby clothes. Since it's late, I don't expect to hear back till tomorrow morning at the soonest. So I'm startled when a dialogue box pops open.

Hey, Bethie!

Manny, do not call me that!

It's your name.

Do you have a death wish?

LOL. U R 2 funE

What do you want?

He would have just sent me another email if he didn't want something. Manny's generous soul often comes with a price.

Since U offered, I want 2 interview @ celebrity.

What celebrity?

Philippe.

U R nuts!!!!!

Only few ?'s

No can do.

Plllllllz!!!!

He's 2 famous. I haven't even talked 2 him.

What about your friends?

My hands pause over the keyboard. Amerie has done more than just talk with Philippe, but no way am I telling that to *read all about it!* Manny. I don't tell him Amerie's name, either, although I admit to having a friend on the contest committee and offer to ask one question for him.

Manny counters with three questions.

We compromise on two.

Then I close the chat window and reopen the attachment about Jay. I print out the one photo that's different from all the others; it shows what I think is the real Jay. I study his face, seeing past the cocky grin to the dark depths of his eyes and wonder what he's thinking, who he really is behind those deep eyes.

That familiar "finding" feeling hits me. There's an internal tug, like a hand pulling me away from the computer and out of the room. Clutching the printout, I go with the feeling. I follow my unseen guide through the hall, up the staircase, and into my attic room.

When the door shuts behind me, the thud snaps me out of my trance.

What was that about? I sit on a stool by my bed. I'm breathing hard and sweating as if I've been running. I stare down at the printout, then shake my head, annoyed with myself. Why am I letting this guy get to me? He's rude, arrogant, and a criminal.

As I'm wondering why he bugs me so much, I hear a noise outside my window. I'm on the third floor, so I assume it's just a bird—until I look over through my sliding door. Someone is on my balcony.

It's Jay.

SIXTEEN

I resist the urge to throw something at him, because why break my own window?

Instead I stomp over and pull the door open with a fierce yank. "You have a lot of nerve coming here!" I say furiously.

"Hey, Thorn." Jay is draped in his black Reaper clothes, except for the gloves and smiley face ski mask. "Nice room. Can I come in?"

"No!" I try to slide the door shut but he sticks his expensive sneaker in the way.

Then he puts up his hands defensively as if he thinks I might try to push him over the balcony, which is a real possibility. "Truce," he says. "I just want to talk."

"Ever heard of a phone? Get off my balcony!"

"Why the hostility?" He puts on an innocent expression, but I'm not fooled.

"You know what you did! And I do, too. Your minion gave it away by laughing at the scene of your crime."

"I don't know what you're talking about, and I do not have minions." He pushes further into my room, so our faces are only angry breaths apart.

"Your Jay-Clones," I spit out. "Wiley was there, gloating over your tagging. You make me sick! Hurting someone who never wronged anyone else is beyond low! K.C. is the sweetest, kindest, most generous guy I know. Why tag his car?"

"I didn't."

"Wiley thinks you did."

"Wiley doesn't know anything. He has no idea I'm the Reaper."

"Yeah, right," I say skeptically. "How can your closest friends not know?"

"If they did, they'd turn me in—after they beat the crap out of me. They hate the Reaper." He gestures to the ski mask half hanging from his coat pocket, where only half a yellow smile shows. "Mason, Wiley, and Keith are okay, but Danny—he's my third cousin—has a mean streak. Last year he was one of the Reaper's targets."

"Your own cousin?" I'm not sure if I'm disgusted or impressed.

"He deserved it. He used his girlfriend as a punching bag, then when she dumped him he trashed her rep in online videos. So the Reaper cast him in a video on how to treat ladies with respect." He grins. "That video passed a million hits on YouTube."

"Why are you telling me this? Aren't you afraid it'll get back to your *friends*?" I emphasize the last word in an accusing way.

"I know you can be trusted," he says.

"Don't you mean *blackmailed*?"

"Whatever works."

My hand grips the sliding door forcefully, keeping him out of my room. I don't want to talk to him, but I'm both intrigued and reconsidering my plan to shove him off the balcony. I'm not ready to invite him in.

"I haven't gone to NB High long, so I don't know much about what happened last year," I admit. "I didn't even know about the Grin Reaper until this week. A lot of things don't make sense. Your friends look up to you so much, yet you don't confide in them. Why hang with people you don't trust?"

"It's complicated."

"That's the vague sort of non-reply I'd expect from you. How about being honest for a change?"

He bites his lower lip, which I notice is slightly chapped. There's a tiny scar, too, at the edge of his lips, giving him a ghost half-smile even though he's scowling. He's so close I smell his earthy scent—sweat, and citrus from soap or shampoo.

"You want the truth?" he asks quietly.

"It would be a refreshing change."

"I had nothing to do with what happened to K.C.'s car—but I know who did it."

My fingers slip from the sliding door as I reel back. "How do you know?"

"I told you I have ways of finding out things. When someone hurts a decent guy like K.C., I don't sit around doing nothing. I gather facts—then I make plans. I'll tell you more if you let me inside."

"I've been told to never let strangers into my home,"

"And you always do exactly what you're told," he says sarcastically.

"Of course. My mother is a minister, you know, so I'm a model citizen."

He laughs, and I can't help but smile, too.

I glance behind him into darkness. "Why even come here?"

"To give you an invitation."

"Sorry, but I don't do proms."

He laughs. "I'd be disappointed if you did."

"What's the invitation?"

"The Grin Reaper is going after the guy who tagged K.C.'s car. Tonight. Want to come along?"

His words are more seductive than poetry or music. Not in a romantic way—in a vengeful way. Although I have to admit there's something roguishly sexy about Jay that adds a thrill when I answer, "yes."

So I invite him into my room.

"All this yours?" He gestures to my living room, which opens into a bedroom with a peaked ceiling, the kitchenette, and my private bathroom.

"As much as a rented house can be. My parents want the younger kids closer to them, so I lucked out and got the attic. It's drafty, with old plumbing and a toilet that doesn't always flush. But it's great to finally have my own bedroom."

"Not a bedroom: a suite." He gives a low appreciative whistle. "Sweet."

I shrug, not believing for a minute that the son of a wealthy judge is impressed with my ramshackle farmhouse.

"Sit there." I point to the sagging couch which came with the house. "I'm going to change my clothes."

"Can I watch?" he teases.

"Only if you want to get kicked somewhere that will hurt very badly."

"Tempting offer but I'll pass." He shifts his hands to cover his lap.

"Good idea." I'm smiling as I shut my bedroom door behind me.

What does a girl wear on a Vigilante Night Out?

I open drawers and search my wardrobe, settling on black jeans, a dark blue knit top, and a black jacket. I shut off the warning in my head that this is insanity squared by stupidity. I refuse to think of consequences. Instead I remember K.C.'s stricken face staring at his ravaged car. And I lust for revenge.

When I step out into the brittle icy air on my balcony, I blink into inky night until my vision adjusts. The sky is blanketed in dark clouds that shut out the stars, and if there's a moon, it's hidden, too. I tighten my jacket, then look down to see how Jay got up to my balcony. He gestures to a grapple hook rope attached to the balcony rail.

"Climbing was easy," he explains.

"Not bad for an amateur."

"Amateur?" He snorts. "You got something better?"

"Live and learn," I say with a swagger as I reach down for my silk ladder.

I attach the ladder to the rail and toss it over the balcony; it unfolds with the grace of silken wings. Gripping the rail, I fling myself over, my feet catching on the rungs of the fabric ladder. Then I climb down as if the silky cloth is a sturdy staircase.

"Not bad for an amateur." Grinning, Jay tosses his grapple hook and rope to the ground, then follows me down my silken ladder.

I pull the string to roll up the ladder, then follow Jay through the back gate. We hurry down our long dirt driveway to the country road, where only a dim light from our porch cuts through the night.

"Where are we going?" I ask, with a curious glance up and down the deserted street.

"Seven miles east."

"Like that tells me anything."

"Patience," he says.

"Not one of my traits."

"I'll explain all soon."

"You'd better," I tell him.

His strides are long and quick, making me half-run so I don't lose him. I consider asking him to slow down, but that would come off as weak—which I'm not. So I take two steps to his every step. After what has to be a mile, I'm breathing hard. When he said we were going seven miles, I didn't think he meant by foot. I'm relieved when he stops at a teal green sedan parked on the road.

"This is your car?" I expected him to drive the latest model pickup, like most guys at Nevada Bluff High.

"No. My father's." There's a hint of bitterness in his tone.

"He's okay with your using it?"

"He's okay with anything I do—as long as I keep up my GPA and stay out of his way." Jay shrugs, then opens the passenger door for me in a gentlemanly gesture. The door shuts behind me and there's a click of the lock as I slip into plush leather.

He twists the key in the ignition. The engine is soft as a kitten's purr and the heavy doors are soundproof; it's like we're shut off from the world. Jay doesn't turn on the headlights for a few miles. It's eerie to drive with no lights, only the faint red and blue glow from the dashboard. When he flips the lights on, the dashboard flashes with complex dials and buttons. I suspect this deluxe luxury sedan could drive itself.

"Now we can talk." He leans back comfortably in his seat and steers with only two fingers on the wheel.

"I only want to hear the truth."

"You think I'd lie?" He lifts his brows, offended.

"It seems likely, considering how good you are at it."

"I swear I won't lie to you," he says with a cross-the-heart gesture. "If you ask something I can't talk about, I just won't answer."

"Fair enough. So start with the name of the tagger." Anger flares as I remember the broken-winged hood eagle and K.C.'s stricken face. "Who is he?"

"Clive Farnway."

163

I search my memory but come up blank. "Don't know him."

"You don't want to." Jay replies. "But you've probably seen his truck—super-sized tires, gold hubcaps, fully loaded and lifted up high enough to drive over a bull without getting pierced by its horns."

"That monstrosity?" I scowl. "It always takes up three parking places."

"That's Clive for you—greedy as all get-out. And a mean bastard."

"What does he have against K.C.?"

"Nothing personal. I doubt he even knows K.C. With Clive, it's all about cars. He's a car snob. If K.C.'s car had been the latest-model truck, Clive would have been cool with it. But he considers all old cars junk—even a vintage classic."

"You're saying Clive attacked K.C.'s car because it wasn't good enough for him?" I ask angrily.

"Clive is picky about what's acceptable for the student parking lot. This isn't the first time he's tagged a car." Jay's lip scar stretches into a dead-serious line. "But it will be his last."

I like the dangerous edge to his tone. Jay and I are on the same side now—at least for tonight.

"So what's the plan?" I ask him. "Are we going to beat Clive until he looks like dog meat?"

"Violence isn't my style," Jay says as the darkness folds around us. "My punishments suit the crime."

"Like what?"

"Strike Clive where it'll hurt worse than anything physical." Jay's grin widens. "We're going after his truck."

SEVENTEEN

Clive lives in an area of expensive ranch homes where the fencing is plastic and the horses are pedigreed. We park a few blocks away and start walking.

"What if someone sees us?" I ask when I spot a neighborhood watch sign and security lights glaring from driveways.

"We pretend to be lovers out for an evening walk."

"Don't make me ill."

Jay chuckles. "Pretend I'm the hottest guy you know and you're wild for my body."

I roll my eyes. "I'm not that good an actress."

"Then we should rehearse now. First step is holding my hand." His words throw out a challenge.

I don't back down, reminding myself I'm doing this for K.C.

The callused touch of Jay's hand surprises me. I'd expected that a preppy guy who lettered in golf—not a rough sport like football—would have soft skin. Besides, as the Reaper, he wears gloves. His hands are tan, with long fingers with a firm grip. There's a ring on his left hand, a large smooth stone with multifaceted angles. It's too dark to see what kind of stone, but I'm guessing something expensive like a diamond or ruby; a ring easily identified, which explains why the Reaper wears gloves.

His voice breaks into my thoughts. "Are you going out with K.C.?"

I rock back on my heels as if thrown off balance. "Why do you want to know?"

"Curious. Is he your boyfriend?"

My cheeks warm. "Don't be stupid. K.C.'s just a friend."

"A friend that lives with you," he points out.

"Not with me—with my very large family. K.C. doesn't even sleep in the house. He has the room over the garage."

"He's a boarder?"

"More like an adopted brother," I say fondly. "When I met him, he was living out of his car. He's had some bad breaks but he's working hard to make something of himself. He helps my parents by fixing our car and doing occasional babysitting. He has a job after school and is saving for his own place, but it'll take a while because he sends money home to his sister."

"Sounds like a saint."

"He's just a nice guy," I say defensively.

"And I'm not," he says, in a way that could be an apology or a boast.

"Not much. When we first met you pushed me down, stole my backpack, and tossed it in a Dumpster."

"I needed to hurry back to class so I could anonymously leave a note saying where to find Bruce Gibson. I only dumped the backpack to get rid of you. I felt bad about that."

"I thought you weren't going to lie," I accuse him.

"It's the truth. You might not believe it, but the Grin Reaper evens the score around here. Nice kids are an endangered species and need protecting."

"But what makes you their protector?" I retort.

"I can't stand bullies winning and nice kids being victims. Like what happened to your friend." Jay arrogantly lifts his chin. "Do you think what I do is wrong?"

"Well … not so much anymore. I understand wanting to help the underdog. But why sneak around in a mask? If you know who's guilty, why not go to a teacher, or to the sheriff for more serious things?"

"Knowing and proving aren't the same. Besides, have you met Sheriff Hart?"

"Unfortunately, yes," I say ruefully. "I get the feeling he thinks all teens are guilty until proven innocent."

"Yeah." Jay nods. "If you're under age, you're under suspicion. He's not corrupt like a lot of officials around here, but he can be as dense as winter fog. You need to smack him with hard evidence to get his attention. Since I don't have proof that Clive tagged K.C.'s car, there's no point in telling the sheriff. I'll get my own justice."

"Like your name."

"Justice is my father's name." He stops walking. My eyes have adjusted to the semi-darkness, so when he stares at me,

I can see every curve and edge of his face. "You know what my mom used to say?"

I shake my head.

"'Don't expect life to be fair and you'll never be disappointed. But when a rare miracle of justice occurs, be grateful.'"

"I like that," I tell him. "Your mom sounds cool."

"She was." He glances down at the ground, then back up at me. "I learned the hard way not to wait around for miracles. I create my own justice."

The angry passion in his tone surprises me. Did something happen to his mother? Is that what drove him to become the Reaper? I want to ask, only there's an uneasy tension between us. Being so close, talking like old friends instead of... well, I'm not sure what we are now. Not friends, but no longer enemies.

"We're away from security lights." I walk ahead of him. "If we stay in the shadows, no one will see us."

"Yeah." He points up a rolling hillside. "Clive lives up there."

I look past the lush green lawn, which seems oddly out of place in this rural setting. I hear whinnies of horses from a pasture surrounded by pale white fencing that looms ghost-like in the dark. Golden lights twinkle from a sprawling two-story house—not a farmhouse, more like a mansion.

"Now what?" I ask.

"We hope there aren't any vicious guard dogs."

"Comforting thought." I listen carefully, hearing nothing except the wind and neighing from the horses.

"I didn't have much time to check things out," Jay says almost apologetically. "Only a quick drive-by of the area and a trip to the hardware store."

"Why the hardware store?"

"Supplies."

"Where are they?" I gesture at his empty hands.

"In the car for later."

He stops in front of a livestock gate and unhooks the latch. After holding the gate open for me to step through, he latches it behind us. We make our way cautiously along the fence line, creeping low until we reach the red barn.

"What are you planning?" I ask, suddenly nervous when it occurs to me that he might be an arsonist. "Nothing that hurts animals?"

"No animals will be harmed in the course of my actions tonight."

"Then what are you going to do?"

He puts his finger to his lips. "No more talking."

I hear squawking from chickens but no barking, which is a small relief. We move in the shadows, nearing the barn with its strong odor of manure and the low sound of moo-ing. We pass the barn and continue toward the house. Are we going to break into Clive's home?

But Jay stops in front of a large metal building, which I thought was another barn until he whispers it's a garage. "Clive's into big, expensive toys." He reaches out for the large double doors and pulls the curved metal handle. But nothing happens.

"It's locked," I say, both disappointed and relieved.

"I can handle it," he assures me as he reaches into his coat pocket for a slim cloth case the size of a wallet. He slides it open to reveal tiny metal picks. I watch in fascination as he tries different picks, poking until there's a click and the door opens.

I'm hit with a strong grease-and-oil smell as I stare into a vast room that's more spacious and loaded with equipment than the auto shop K.C. works at. There are work tables covered in tools, a mechanical lift fixed to the ceiling, and in the center, like a prize on display, Clive's gleaming truck.

Even if Jay hadn't already told me, it's obvious that this truck is Clive's heart. Excitement rips through me as I anticipate Jay's next move. I'm puzzled, though, because he doesn't have any paint, knives, or bomb-making equipment with him. I follow him slowly, only able to make out vague shapes in the darkness.

"How strong are you?" Jay asks when he reaches the truck.

"Stronger than I look."

"You'll need to be."

He climbs up on the driver's side of the truck and swings open the door. A light flashes. I worry someone will see us, but Jay turns off the inner light and we're enveloped in blackness.

I can't see what he's doing, but he's done before I can ask. He jumps out of the truck and goes to the large entry doors, pushing them wide open.

"Jay!" I call out, alarmed. "Someone might see us!"

"The house is dark, and the porch light faces the other

direction. Besides, we're going to be quiet. I've fixed the steering wheel and the truck ready to roll. All we have to do is push it out of here and once it's far enough away from the house, I'll start the engine."

"Are you totally insane? Grand theft auto!"

"We're not stealing the truck, just borrowing it."

"Of course. That makes it okay," I say sarcastically.

"Chill. We won't get caught."

Easy for him to say, with his rich daddy to bail him out and arrange to have all charges dropped with a magic-wand-wave of a checkbook—while I'd still be in jail. I'm ready to refuse until I remember K.C. and the sick slurs on his car. When Jay leads me to the back of the truck and says "Push," I don't argue.

Every creak and groan of the truck sounds a thousand times louder. And I imagine sirens blaring on their way to arrest us. But I push on, the wheels rolling smoothly on concrete, then more slowly on hard dirt. I'm sweating now, too, pushing with all my might.

We pause when the truck starts to veer the wrong direction, and Jay jumps back inside (the light no longer flashes on). He's back out quickly and we push until the truck sinks into darker shadows. The ground dips and the truck rolls faster—much too fast! My hands slip and I half-stumble to the ground, then hurry to catch up. The truck levels out and we're closer to the livestock gate.

"This should be far enough," Jay says, then he jumps inside the truck, gesturing for me to join him. He keeps the lights off but fiddles with some hanging wires and the engine starts up with a powerful purr, like a caged tiger released into the night. We're through the gate and out onto the main road.

We return to Jay's car and he tosses me the keys, then tells me to follow while he drives the truck to the high school.

The main part of town is quiet, with only a few cars on the road and most businesses shut up for the night. The high school parking lot is locked and has security lights. Jay flips a U-turn, directing me to park on the street near the school entrance. I climb up next to him in the truck and we leave his car behind.

We ride in silence for about a mile, questions about his plan screaming in my head. But I'm more curious about him. What turns a rich kid into a vigilante?

So I ask him.

I think he's going to pretend not to hear me, but then he says, "It just happened."

"What exactly?" I persist. "How did it begin?"

He gnaws on his lower lips, staring out across the dashboard as if seeing into the past instead of the deserted road ahead. "I've never told anyone."

"I've never committed grand larceny. But I'm here."

The scar on the corner of his mouth deepens when he grins. "I find that really hot in a girl."

"You know what I find hot in a guy?" I look him directly in his dark eyes. "Honesty."

"Good luck with that," he says bitterly.

"So don't tell me anything. I didn't think you would anyway."

He stares ahead as if totally focused on driving. But his fingers grip the steering wheel, both hands tight in a strangle hold as if he's wrestling with himself.

"It's because of my father," Jay blurts out.

I nod for him to continue.

"The Honorable Justice Blankenship was never very honorable, but my mother was like his conscience, and so he was a good judge until she died."

I want to say "I'm sorry" only it doesn't seem like enough, so I say nothing.

"My father turned bitter and got sucked into the power of his position. I became just another asset to him, like black ink instead of red on his financial accounts. He gave me anything I asked for—private instructors in martial arts, guitar, golf, fencing, and more. I thought this was his way of showing he cared, and I pretended not to notice his dishonest dealings. But then that kid hurt the school dog."

"Rune told me about that."

"Everyone knew who did it, and he even got caught on a security camera. But his dad knew my dad and the charges were dropped. I went to my father and accused him of being bought. You know what he said?"

I shake my head.

"He bragged about it, saying it was easy money. When I called him corrupt, he told me this was a valuable lesson about how things worked in the adult world. 'You're a spineless bleeding heart just like your mother,' he said. That night, the Grin Reaper struck for the first time. Martial arts training made it easy to overpower the little dog-abuser creep. I wanted to kill him—I really did. Lucky for him, I only wrote on his head."

"And left a smiley face sticker."

"About that sticker..." Jay chuckles darkly. "I didn't leave it."

"What? But then who did?"

"I don't know how it got there—probably dropped by a little kid. But when rumors spread and someone came up with the name the Grin Reaper, I started leaving the symbol on purpose."

"Big bad Grin Reaper," I say with a teasing shudder.

"You'd better believe it." He flashes me an exaggerated grin. "Hold on, things are going to get interesting very soon."

The truck jerks right as he makes a sudden turn onto a road that's familiar, although I don't place it at first. We're surrounded by rugged hills, dipping and curving along high desert. A faint moon peaks out from clouds, slicing a silvery trail across cactus, rocks, and weeds with mysterious beauty that touches something deep inside me. My gaze is drawn to a lone barn in the horizon, its steeply pitched roof sparking my memory. This is the same route I took a few days ago—when I found the grave.

I tense, anticipating a left turn through the pale skeletons of the housing development, but Jay takes a right onto a darkened road and slows to a stop. Nearly finished homes rise around us. I can make out a few streetlights, but they're dark. The street dead-ends; it's an empty, unfinished cul-de-sac, very private with no nosy neighbors.

Jay reaches in the back for a bag that clatters metallically as he jumps onto the road. "Come on, Thorn," he calls. "We've got to do this fast."

"Do what?" I ask, coming around to stand beside him. I eye the bag curiously.

"Give Clive's truck a new paint job." He opens the bag and pulls out a can of spray paint. "What do you think of the color pink?"

We work under the soft glow of a flashlight Jay has propped up on the pavement. The paint smell is strong but not unpleasant. Jay's thought of everything, and even has coveralls and latex gloves ready.

He shows me four cans of pink paint, plus a yellow and black. Tossing me a pink can, he says, "Go for it!"

Paint hisses like angry snakes shooting from our fingers. Jay starts at the front so I go to the back, flourishing pink across the truck bed, tires and windows. I'm on my second can when I feel something smack my arm and look up to find Jay grinning at me, armed with a paint can. "Oops," he says with a laugh.

"You did that on purpose!" There's a bright pink streak on my coverall.

"Me?" He says in mock innocence.

He's such a liar, and I'm laughing as I spray him back. Bull's eye! A pink heart across his chest!

"That gives me an idea!" I say, and end our paint war by turning back to the truck. Almost ever inch of it is covered with pink, but that's not good enough. I pick up a can of black paint and spray a heart on the driver's side door.

"Nice touch," Jay approves. "But don't forget the other side."

So I paint more black hearts.

And while I'm doing this, Jay takes a yellow can to the front of the truck. He aims at the hood, drawing a giant circle. Then he switches to black paint for the inside of the circle.

"Perfect! A smiley face," I say, laughing.

My laughter dies like a vampire with a stake through its heart when I glance over Jay's shoulder and see bright lights. There's something familiar about the shape of the distant vehicle. "It's the sheriff's car!" I exclaim.

Jay only pauses long enough to swear then he's moving fast, tossing near-empty cans back in the bag and scrambling to the truck. "Hurry! Get in!" he calls to me.

Then we're off.

I'm turned around, staring out the back window (although it's very hard to see through the pink), watching the far-away lights. They don't come closer, so maybe I was wrong about it being the sheriff. Regardless, we got away.

A short while later, we reach Nevada Bluff High. We glance around furtively to make sure no one is watching, then leave the truck just far enough away from the security cameras but close enough that no one can miss the bright candy pink. We're back in Jay's car and out of there so fast my head spins.

Adrenaline rushes through me, and I look over at Jay. He's nothing like I expected, and I have a crazy urge to reach over and grasp his hand. Then I realize how dumb this is—he's not any more my type than I'm his. Sure, he's cool, wanting to help people in sort of a Zorro way. But he's rich, too, and he lives in a gated area of Nevada Bluff that would never invite me in.

Still, I like being near him, and it was exciting breaking the law with him. I wonder what a real date with Jay would be like... would he want to kiss me when he dropped me off? My friends and his friends would be shocked to see us together: Popular Prep + Goth Girl. For shock value alone, it might be worth trying.

When we turn onto in driveway, I notice that my house—which was dark when I left—is now ablaze with lights.

I'm in deep, deep trouble.

EIGHTEEN

Jay drops me off a short distance away and I walk slowly to my doom. I could sneak around the back, but what's the use? Bracing myself, I enter through the front door.

I expect it to be bad. *It's worse.*

While Mom looks upward and mouths, "Thank God," she doesn't move to hug me. Dad steps forward, his face mottled with fury as he wags a pointed finger in my face and shouts, "WHERE HAVE YOU BEEN?"

What am I supposed to say? *I was out with the Grin Reaper. We trespassed, broke into a building, stole a car, then spray-painted it pink.* Dad would probably haul my ass off to jail before I could wipe the tiny specks of pink off my boots.

So I refuse to answer.

Mom's eyes are red-rimmed. She steps forward and puts her hand on my arm. "Are you okay? You can tell us anything," she assures me.

No, I can't. Not even when I'm old and have kids of my own.

"Honey, this is serious." Mom sounds emotionally and physically drained. "We didn't know who to call—you never bring friends home. We were going to call the sheriff if you didn't show up. We were so worried."

I try to hide my gasp at the thought of another encounter with Sheriff Hart. The seriousness of what almost happened makes my legs weak.

Dad doesn't look worried, only furious. Since I still won't talk, he starts shouting again. When he says he called Skarla's house looking for me and woke up her grandparents, I'm mad, too.

"I can't believe you did that!" I exclaim. "This is exactly why I don't tell you who my friends are. I'm not a little kid who needs to be checked up on. I'm almost eighteen! I'm sorry I lost track of time, but I was safe and you should trust me."

"You've proved you can't be trusted," Dad retorts. "Even K.C. didn't know how to contact your friends. Another five minutes and we would have reported you missing. This type of irresponsible, secretive behavior ends now." He gets close to my face. "You will give us a list of your friends, with their phone numbers. If your friends want to see you, they can damn well come here. You will be driven to and from school every day. And your driving privileges are suspended indefinitely. Do you understand?"

I want to argue, but I've never seen Dad this mad, not even when he lost his job. He doesn't wait for my answer anyway, whirling away and storming out of the room.

Mom and I are left alone. She stares at me sadly. "Why do you make everything so difficult?" she asks softly.

She looks so miserable that I long to put my arms around her and say I'm sorry. But I stand stiff, my anger sparking ugly emotions. "It just happens."

"This isn't the first time you've disappeared with no explanation. Don't you have anything to say for yourself?" She rubs her forehead.

"Not really."

"Can't you at least try to be part of our family?"

"Do I have a choice?"

"There are always choices, Beth Ann."

"My name's Thorn," I say coolly. "That's the real issue here, isn't it? You can't stand that I'm goth. You and Dad want me to be a perfect little minister's daughter. I saw your expression when I interrupted your tea with the church ladies. You were ashamed of me."

"That's not true!"

"You didn't introduce me and gestured for me to leave."

"We were busy discussing church business."

"You wanted me out of there because I embarrass you. I'm a disgrace to the family, just like that letter said."

Mom rocks back on her heels. "What letter?"

"Don't pretend you don't know. I accidentally found it in your desk."

"You were snooping in my desk?" she accuses.

"Add it to the list of how horrible I am, just like the letter said."

"There wasn't only one letter—there were three. And

for your information, I've thrown them away." Mom's swift fury surprises me. "I will not be threatened by an interfering busybody!"

"But you could lose your job and the house."

"Then we'll move again. No one tells me how to raise my kids."

"Even your most difficult kid?" I ask ruefully.

"Especially her." Mom's face softens and she reaches out to stroke my hair; of course it's not my real hair, but a black wig with red streaks. "I won't say I agree with everything you do, but I respect your independence. Even as a toddler, you always did things your own way—climbing instead of crawling, running rather than walking, and once you started talking, there was no slowing your questions. You still question everything—which is a wonderful part of who you are."

"I thought you hated all this?" I gesture from my head to my army boots.

"No—although I do miss your lovely blond hair," she says with a wistful sigh. "But it's my job to raise you, not change you. And if anyone else tries, they'll have to get past me first."

I'm touched by her words and feel closer to her than I have in a long time. Too bad I can't be honest about where I was tonight. Instead I give her a hug.

"You don't hate me?" I ask softly.

"I could never hate you."

"So I'm not in trouble any more?"

"Don't push your luck." She playfully tugs a black strand

of my wig. "Everything your dad says goes. You're grounded until you're at least thirty."

"Tomorrow I'm auditioning for the Singing Star contest," I remind her. "I'll have to stay after school."

"That won't be a problem."

"Great, because I really—"

"You didn't let me finish," Mom cuts in pointedly. "It won't be a problem because I'm going to be in the audience. I can't wait to see my daughter on stage."

Then she kisses my cheek and strolls casually out of the room.

Just great, I think grimly. As if performing won't be stressful enough, I'll have a parental guard in the audience.

I fall asleep to dreams of myself on stage completely naked with only my guitar to hide behind. Then my guitar vanishes—and I wake up dripping with sweat. *I have to get out of the contest*, I think desperately. Call in sick? Break my arm? Join the Marines?

There aren't any more nightmares, but I toss and turn until finally, at three a.m., I snap on my bedside lamp and pick up my guitar, strumming a bittersweet melody that would make a great ballad if I could actually write lyrics. I notice a speck of pink on my hand and wonder how it got through my gloves. My mind jumps from Jay to the pink truck to what my mother said, then circles back to Jay.

I remember the warmth of Jay's callused hands and how his dark eyes shone when he grinned. Will he even talk to me at school now, or stride by with his pals like I'm invisible? Not that I care ... I'm just curious. It's like Jay is two different people—the arrogant prep and the avenging Grin Reaper. But it's this odd combination that intrigues me.

After I put my guitar away and settle down in bed, my brain still won't shut off.

Does doing something bad for a good reason make me a bad or good person?

Maybe the real question is, what kind of person do I want to be?

A vigilante like Jay? No, definitely not. I only went out with Jay tonight because of K.C. It won't ever happen again.

I sink into a deep sleep. It doesn't last long, though, because I wake up early.

Studying myself in the mirror, I see a faint resemblance to Mom. Everyone says I take after her—in looks, anyway. We're both blue-eyed blonds with freckles and skin too pale to tan without burning. But Mom thrives on being with people and truly believes that everyone has some good in them. I limit my trust to a few friends. Mom trusts everyone—even me. She may not approve of my goth style, but she doesn't criticize. And as a reward for her big heart, she may lose her job.

I can't shake an uneasy guilt as I take a very hot shower and wash off specks of pink paint and faded makeup. Instead of taking out my makeup case and applying mascara, eyeliner, eyebrow pencil, foundation, blush, and dusky plum eye shadow, I only dab on peach frost lip-gloss. Then I blow-dry and brush my blond hair till it shines in waves to my shoulders.

Next I take off my piercings—tongue, ears, eyebrow—

leaving only the tiny diamond in my belly button. I leave my army boots in my wardrobe and don't drape my wrists with silver bangles. Instead of midnight-black clothes, I slip into my fringed pink skirt, lace up my pink ankle boots, and tighten the peasant blouse with a plain white belt. Then I top it off with the pink cowgirl hat.

And when I look in the mirror again, I see Beth Ann.

There's no trace of Thorn.

———

Walking downstairs to breakfast, I'm holding my breath, nervous like when I first played my guitar in front of the CCCs. I'm relieved that only my father and K.C. are at the dining table. Dad is buttering toast and nearly stabs himself when he sees me.

"I—I hardly recognize you!" Dad's knife clatters on the table.

"Me either," I say.

Dad puts down his half-buttered toast. "You look good."

I'm relieved he's talking to me, so I just nod.

K.C. hasn't stopped staring. He stabs a chunk of frozen waffle with his fork and pops it into his mouth, wisely saying nothing.

"Skarla gave me the costume." I pop a frosted tart into the toaster. "For the contest."

"Oh, yes." Dad smiles at me for the first time in months. "Your mother mentioned a singing contest."

"I'm not really singing, only playing guitar and doing some harmonizing. We're auditioning today."

"Well … good luck." Dad clears his throat and looks away uncomfortably. "Your mother said she'd drive you home, so I'll drive you to school."

"Why don't I take her?" K.C. offers. "My Ranchero is still at the shop but my other car works. No reason for you to drive when I have to go to school anyway."

Dad hesitates, then nods. He has a soft spot for K.C.

A short time later, I slip into K.C.'s car, the door creaking a complaint, and when I catch a glimpse of myself in his rearview mirror, I think I've gone back in time and am twelve-year-old Beth Ann.

"I'm parking on the street," K.C. says as we near the school. "I don't need a repeat of yesterday."

"The tagger won't bother you again," I say, then shut my mouth quickly.

"Why not?"

"He'd be stupid to try it."

"Do you know something I don't?"

I twist a strand of blond hair around my finger. "I just think today will be full of surprises."

He starts to reply—until he looks past me out my window. "Why are all those people crowding around that … ohmygod! That truck is pink!"

"Is it?" I peer out the window all casual-like. In the bright morning light, the truck is such a bright pink it's like it's blushing. And the round yellow smiley face sends a message that Clive won't easily forget.

"I recognize that truck!" K.C. exclaims. "It's Clive Farnway's! The tagger got him, too!"

"Or maybe he *is* the tagger," I say mysteriously, but then I refuse to say any more.

"Why would he tag his own truck?" K.C. pulls into a parking spot on the street, a slow realization dawning on his face. "The smiley face! It was the Grin Reaper!"

"Wow. You think so?"

"You're not fooling me, Thorn." K.C. points at me accusingly. "Does this have anything to do with why you were gone last night?"

"Don't be delusional," I say, but I'm sure my cheeks are as pink as Clive's truck. I grab my guitar and escape before K.C. can ask me anything else.

When I meet Rune at my locker, she looks right past me without any sign of recognition. Then her gaze flickers back. Her mouth gapes open.

"Yeah, it's me," I say.

"But you look ... so pink! It's like a pink invasion! First Clive's truck, and now you."

"Scary, huh?" I joke.

She plants her hands on her hips. "What's going on?"

"I'm wearing my CCC costume," I tell her as I spin my locker combination.

"But why look like a bubblegum explosion all day? You could have changed into it right before you perform."

"It's easier this way."

She frowns. "You're not even wearing makeup."

"Lip gloss," I smack my lips. "And this is my real hair."

"I prefer your wigs."

"Wigs get old after a while. You know I'm allergic to hair dye."

"Whatever." She slams her locker shut. "Just so you know, I'm still mad at you."

"You should be. I've been a horrible friend. I'm surprised you're still speaking to me."

"I considered making you grovel and beg for forgiveness."

"So why let me off so easily?"

"I can't afford to lose another friend."

"Another?" I arch a brow.

"Amerie." Rune rakes her fingers through her now jet-black hair. "I finally got her on the phone last night and warned her not to date Philippe. I did some online research and had a long list of girls he dated. The worst was a girl named Rebecca, who tried to commit suicide after he dumped her."

"Seriously?" I can't imagine giving a guy so much power over my emotions.

Rune nods. "Rebecca spent months recovering in a mental health center—all because of Philippe. I warned Amerie not to trust him, told her he'll break her heart. I was trying to be a good friend, but you know what she did? Hung up on me! I'm through trying to help her."

"Philippe will leave when the contest ends," I say as we walk to the intersection where we'll go in different directions. "Then Amerie will return to normal."

"Not if he screws her over—literally. What if she gets pregnant?"

"She wouldn't be dumb enough not to take precautions."

"But she's not acting rational!" Rune stamps her black boot. "She told me she'd been saving herself for the perfect guy and now that she's found him, they're going to be together forever. She's fallen so hard that when he dumps her, she'll go psycho like Rebecca."

"If Amerie falls, we'll be there to pick up the pieces," I say, which results in the first real smile from Rune.

Homeroom is torturous due to all the stares. Whispers and rumors swirl around me. One girl who has sat next to me since the beginning of school asks if I'm a new student.

I get a similar reaction in all of my classes. No one recognizes me, and a few mistake me for a new student. I like shocking people, but this is just annoying. I hurry through the halls with my head down.

"Thorn!" I hear as I'm rushing to fourth period, and I'm so stunned that someone recognizes me, I whirl around.

Skarla, looking like my dark-haired twin in her pink costume, wraps me in a hug before I can push her off. "You're gorgeous!" she exclaims. "That's your natural hair, isn't it? I love it! I'm so honored you did this for our group."

"That's not exactly why I did it," I say. "I really have to get to class…"

"Of course. I just wanted to invite you to a celebration party at my house after auditions."

"You can't be sure we'll make finals."

"Oh, I'm sure. We're fabulous! So can you come?"

"I don't think so." I hesitate. "I'm sort of grounded."

"Your parents will let you go to something this important."

"Yeah, they might." I remember Dad's rare smile at breakfast when he saw me in pink. "I'll talk to them."

"Great. See you at the contest!"

She bounces off with such cheerfulness it's hard to believe she's my top suspect. But I can't forget her hidden stash of baby clothes. Highly suspicious, although not proof she had anything to do with the locket or grave. I need to search her room more thoroughly. If I can find the locket, I'll know for sure.

At lunch, I meet Rune on the cafeteria steps. I tell her that K.C. won't join us since he's working on a history project in the computer center.

"Whatever. Have you heard?" she asks excitedly.

"About the pink truck?" I guess.

"Wasn't it hilarious? But the big news is that everyone is sure the Grin Reaper did it—which means that Clive was the one who tagged K.C.'s car!"

"Why would he do something like that?" I ask innocently.

"I don't know. Maybe because he's a jerk. The smiley face painted on his truck sends out a clear message that this was payback for what he did to K.C. Everyone knows that Clive deserves it, even if they can't prove it."

"It really sucked, what happened to K.C.'s car," I say, anger rising with the memory. "I'm all for getting even with the vermin who did it."

"So you don't hate the Grin Reaper anymore?" Rune teases.

I shrug. If she knew I had a Vigilante Night Out with the Grin Reaper, she's totally freak—and want every detail plus his phone number.

"The Reaper is brilliant. Pink-sweet revenge." Rune sighs. "He's so hot and I just have to meet him. Hurry up and find him for me."

I open my sack lunch, avoiding her gaze. "He's not an easy guy to find."

"But you said you'd recognize his voice."

"It's harder than I thought. Maybe he goes to another school."

"You really think so?" Rune's shoulders slump. "Then it's hopeless. I'll never meet my soul mate."

"You're not missing much."

She purses her purple-lined black lips. "How do you know?"

"I don't. Only guessing."

"You're giving off a serious lying vibe."

I let my blond hair fall across my face, hiding my eyes. "A guy who breaks the law, even for a good cause, must be bad news. You're better off without him."

She sets her iced tea on the step and says, "You *do* know who he is!"

"Not exactly … I mean … " I glance down at my pink cowgirl boots. I'm sick of the lies. "You're right. I do know."

"Who is he?" Rune demands excitedly. "Tell me!"

"I—I can't say."

"Can't or won't?"

"I'd tell you if I could, but I promised him I wouldn't tell."

"A promise to *him* and lies to *me*!" Rune explodes with such fierceness I reel back. "Why would you take his side over mine? Do you care about protecting him more than helping me?"

"No … it's just complicated. I don't even like him."

"But you're lying for him—to your best friend."

"If I were lying, I'd say I didn't know, but I'm telling the truth and admitting I know, but I'm bound by a promise."

"You aren't fooling me. I know what's really going on." Her kohl-shaded eyes narrow in a hostile way that I've never seen directed at me. "You won't tell me because you want him for yourself. You're in love with the Grin Reaper."

NINETEEN

Rune leaves me sitting on the steps, reeling from her accusation. My ham sandwich tastes stale and my butterscotch pudding remains unopened. This is all Jay's fault. I could have explained things to Rune if he hadn't blackmailed me.

The masked Grin Reaper may still seem thrilling to Rune, but if she knew his real identity, she'd be sooo not interested. Last week, Amerie, Rune, and I made a list of lust-worthy fictional characters that we titled "Dudes We'd Do If They Existed." No shock that Amerie put down Harry Potter, Spiderman, and Peter Pan (even though we told her Peter was traditionally acted by a girl on stage). Rune picked Captain Jack Sparrow and Moriarty. I added Dracula, Mr. Hyde, and the evil scientist in the *Rocky Horror Picture Show*. I'm into outrageous dudes with wild hair and wicked attitudes, not a guy handsome enough to be a Disney prince. Sure, Jay is intriguing and I admire his passion for justice.

But not hating him doesn't mean I like him—especially in a romantic way.

When sixth period ends, my thoughts shift to the auditions. My nerves tighten like guitar strings at the thought of being on stage in front of an audience. Music has always been personal for me, a secret refuge that's mine alone.

I really, really don't want to do this...

But I sling my guitar over my shoulder and enter the boisterous, crowded room. Seats are filling fast with parents, teachers, and students. I can hardly move without bumping someone, and all the "Good luck!" calls only add to my anxiety.

Elevated on stage under bright lights, Philippe and his spiraling raven curls are hard to miss. He's leaning forward in conversation with Collette. I can't see his face, but there's tension in his body language like he's no happier to be here than I am. Or maybe Collette gave him bad news, like his latest CD only earned a million not a billion. She's all glam and gorgeous in a plunging-neck scarlet chiffon dress and red stilettos, and doesn't look any older than Philippe. She seems agitated, though, and scowls when she glances across the stage at Amerie. *What's that about?*

I weave my way down to the front rows where contestants have assigned seating. Three pink western hats pop out in the second row. We're seated in performance order, for quick-on, quick-off access. My gaze fixes on the subtle drama unfolding on stage.

Amerie's iridescent fairy wings, tucked delicately behind her shoulders, shimmer like stardust. She glides over to

Philippe, coming up behind him and sliding her arms around his waist. When he turns toward her, the flash of his pearl-white smile could stop a hummingbird in mid-flutter. He gazes at Amerie as if she's the only girl in the room, seemingly unaware that Collette is glowering at both of them.

Amerie glances in my direction and lifts her arm to wave. "Thorn!" She gestures excitedly for me to come over.

I nod, hoping she'll introduce me to Philippe. Not only do I have the two interview questions to ask for Manny, but I want to find out if Philippe is serious about Amerie. There *is* a chance he's sincere and not leading her on—but it's a very slim chance.

When I reach the steps to the stage, Philippe's husky bodyguard blocks my way, but Amerie intervenes. "Richard, she's a friend. Let her pass."

The brawny, shaved-head guy smiles at Amerie, then drops his arms.

"Thorn!" Amerie exclaims. "I hardly recognize you!"

I frown at my bare hands, which are usually bejeweled with wicked rings. "It's for the contest."

"Totally adorable," she says, mischief in her eyes.

"Abominable is more like it."

"Love the pink hat—it's so you!"

"Say that again, Fairy Girl, and I'll rip off your wings."

"No one touches my wings—except my special guy." Amerie's face softens as she looks over at Philippe, who's mobbed by fans at the edge of the stage.

"As long as that's all he touches," I say.

She whispers into my ear. "Not yet, but I'm hopeful."

"Amerie, don't do anything you'll regret."

"I won't." She presses her lips together in a secret smile. "Seriously, Thorn, you look great and I owe you a zillion thanks for rescuing the Cotton Candy Cowgirls. They were good before, but with your sound, they're amazing. You're way better than Priscilla was. The girls know it, too, because when Priscilla asked to come back to the group, Skarla turned her down."

This is news to me. "Priscilla wanted back in?"

"Yeah. But Skarla is too smart to let you go. She's thanked me like a dozen times for hooking you up with the group. You're so talented."

"Well … thanks." Praise isn't something I'm used to, but I've had more of it today than in my whole life before. Looking like a Cowgirl Barbie has changed how everyone acts around me, which makes me act different. I've always believed that appearance doesn't matter, but on some level it must, because how you look is the first clue to others about who you are. So even though I see myself in goth black, others see a Cotton Candy Cowgirl and they like her better.

"—group has such a great sound and it's because of you," Amerie is saying. "I've been bragging to everyone that you're my best friend."

"I'm not your only BFF," I say in a softer voice. "Rune is too."

"Do not speak her name." Amerie stiffens and lifts her chin defiantly.

"She was trying to help because she's worried about you. She's really sorry."

"She should be. But you can see how amazing Philippe is and understand." Her gaze sweeps over to the spiral-haired heartthrob kneeling on the edge of the stage to sign autographs. "I still can't believe he loves me."

"Yeah," I say, with a completely different meaning. I want to drag her away and slap some sense into her lovestruck head. But tact is required. So I tell her about Manny's interview questions and ask for an introduction to Philippe.

"Sure!" Amerie says enthusiastically. "I've already told him about you."

"Nothing good, I hope."

"The worst." She grins. "He's super sweet and he'll answer your questions if I ask him. We have about fifteen minutes before the contest starts."

Amerie drags Philippe away from the mob of squealing fans (mostly girls, but also a few guys and even a teacher). We move to a corner of the stage, out of the bright lights.

He introduces himself. "I'm Philippe."

"Yeah … I know. I mean, who doesn't? I'm Thorn." I'm struck by sudden shyness. It's his grin, I realize with a traitorous heart-flutter. Even I am not completely immune.

"I've never met anyone named Thorn. Cool name."

"My real name isn't Thorn, and yours isn't Philippe."

"So you've discovered my deepest secret," he says, in a teasing flirty way.

"Not a big secret. I saw your junior-year yearbook photo."

"Hideous photo."

"Hideous is a prerequisite for school pictures."

"So true." He grimaces. "If it were possible, I'd burn every yearbook from that forgettable part of my life."

"School can't have been all bad," I say, leading into Manny's first question. "Did you have a favorite teacher?"

"Teachers had it out for me. I skipped school more than I showed up. But there was one teacher who was cool. We talked about big-band era musicians and he was blown away when I showed him my collection of vinyl. He's still working here, too."

"Who?" I ask taking out a pen and paper from my backpack so I don't miss any details for Manny.

"Mr. Sproat."

I nearly fall off the stage. "No way!"

Amerie gasps. "He's the nastiest, rudest teacher ever. He's like the Professor Snape of our school. Everyone hates him."

"Exactly why we got along." Philippe flashes his megawatt smile. "Next question."

"Make it quick," Amerie tells me, pointing to her Tinker Bell watch.

Manny's second question has to do with boxers or briefs, which is boring. So I mentally scratch that question. I watch Amerie touch Philippe's arm, her face luminous with trust and vulnerability. She needs to know that Philippe will crush her heart and devour her like a whipped-cream dessert.

"My next question," I say with a misleading smile, "has to do with your romantic reputation."

"Don't believe trashy tabloids," he tells me.

"Everyone knows you've gone out with gorgeous

actresses and singers. Weren't you engaged to the last American Idol winner?"

"No engagement. But if the right girl comes along, you never know what could happen." He looks meaningfully at Amerie, who blushes happily.

"I heard you had over thirty girlfriends last year?"

"Paparazzi exaggerate everything. If I'm photographed with a girl, it's suddenly all over the news that we're engaged. But I'm very picky about who I go out with and only want to be with someone special like Amerie." He gives Amerie another of those smoldering looks that seems to suck out her brains.

"Was Rebecca special, too?" I say this more like an accusation than a question. He's too perfect to be real. I don't trust him.

"Rebecca?" He pushes his spiral curls behind his shoulders. "I don't know who you're talking about."

"Rebecca Moreno. You met her at a concert in Ohio."

"Nope." He shrugs. "Never heard of her."

"Really?" I say with sharp skepticism. "Even though she traveled on your tour bus until you dumped her and—"

"Philippe!" A woman interrupts with the force of a hurricane.

We turn as Collette sweeps between us with a warm smile, but her icy green eyes are fixed on me. She's been listening and isn't happy with my question.

"Hey, Col. What's up?" Philippe sounds relieved as he turns to his manager.

"Sorry to interrupt, but we're starting soon." She tugs on his hand. "Come with me."

Philippe reaches out to caress Amerie's cheek, then walks off with his manager to a table and chairs at the edge of the stage.

"What was that about, Thorn?" Amerie turns on me. "Why were you being so rude to Philippe?"

I glance down at the wooden floor as if the scuff marks are suddenly fascinating. "I don't know what you mean."

"Oh, yes you do. You're trying to break us up! You don't approve of my going out with Philippe."

"You're right. I don't," I admit.

"I knew it! You're as bad as Rune."

"We don't want you hurt. Philippe is a player and he's too old for you. You deserve better."

"No one is better." She glares. "You and Rune think I'm a stupid little girl who doesn't know anything, but I know that Philippe loves me."

"He's loved a lot of girls and it never ends well."

"It's different with us." Her tone dares me to argue.

I want to argue, but there's no winning when she's blinded by her heart. So I reach out and squeeze her hand. "I just want you to be happy," I say quietly.

"I am very happy—with Philippe," she insists. "Later I'll tell you some of the sweet things he's said to me and you'll understand. But there's no time now. Five minutes! I've got to hustle. I'm rooting for you. Good luck, Thorn. I'll be crossing my fingers that the Cotton Candy Cowgirls makes the finals."

I watch grimly as Amerie flutters back to Philippe.

After that everything is a blur of pep talks and anticipation, waiting for the audition to start. I'm sitting beside Skarla and only half-listen as she goes over the clog sequence with Micqui and Barbee. My guitar is propped between my knees next to my shiny pink boots. I drum my fingers on my metal chair, impatient to get this over with. There are eight acts auditioning today. We're number eight.

First up is Christiana Lee, a tiny freshman who speaks in a squeaky baby-mouse voice, then bellows out like Aretha. *Wow*, I think. She'll be hard to beat. I'm not sure how I feel about this. Am I hoping to win or lose? I honestly don't know.

The next three groups are forgettable. Already forgot their names. Don't care.

Then Jaden Ming struts out dressed like a very tall Elvis. He's in my Spanish class and I purposely always choose the seat behind him because I'm rarely called on to answer questions when hidden from the teacher's view. Jaden rocks out an Elvis song that causes the audience to clap and stomp, including me.

After him is another forgettable act.

Skarla nudges me—the cue that it's time to go backstage. I pick up my guitar and follow the girls around to a side entrance, then we wait in the wings.

I don't see the group before us until we're in position in the wings. When I do see them—four guys wearing blue shirts and pressed dark slacks—I gasp.

The Jay-Clones! I briefly wonder why Jay isn't with them. And of course, they don't call themselves the Jay-

Clones. When Collette announces them as "Four Play," the audience explodes in laughter. Some teachers look angry but no one drags the guys off the stage.

Wiley is on electric guitar, and the brute with the bad temper (what was his name?) plays the drums. And they're good. I mean, really, hot, sizzling, oh-my-sweet-eardrums good.

"We're dead," Barbee whines.

"Dead and buried deep," Micqui groans.

But Skarla says firmly, "We will win. Be positive. Be stars."

When the applause fades for Four Play, the Cotton Candy Cowgirls are on.

I can't say exactly what happens next because I'm in the moment, focused on the music and shutting out the audience. Skarla's powerful voice rings pure and sweet even while she clogs. I harmonize some "la la's" and "ohhhhh's" while strumming. The other girls kick up their clogging heels and my fingers fly. Barbee does a gymnastic flip as a finale, flashing her pink ruffled pettipants, then landing in the splits. The audience roars with applause and gives us a standing ovation.

Bowing, my heart thumping and my head spinning, I realize that I'm smiling. A thrill of pride rushes through me. What an amazing feeling! We leave the stage, jumping and hugging each other. Then we take our seats while the judges consult.

Philippe and Collette huddle at their table, writing and whispering. Five minutes feels like fifty years, but finally

Collette stands and walks to the edge of the stage. Amerie hands her a microphone.

"The results are in," Collette announces.

A hush settles over the audience.

"After watching all your spectacular performances," Collette says dramatically, "we've narrowed it down to the top entrants from both days of auditions. These ten groups will perform one last time on Friday evening—for the grand prize."

The audience titters with squeals and whispers. I've forgotten how to breathe, leaning forward on the edge of my seat.

"The finals will be televised," Collette declares. "The winning performer or group will be awarded five thousand dollars and the chance to perform as the opening act for Philippe's concert in Las Vegas."

Thunderous stomping, clapping, whistling, and screaming. The images whirl through my head. TV! Las Vegas! My mind boggles and I can't even imagine what stardom would be like. I'm terrified ... but tempted.

One-fourth of five thousand dollars would really help my family out.

And when nine groups have been announced, with only one spot remaining, I hold my breath, afraid to think or hope or breathe.

"And the final group to compete is ... " Collette pauses dramatically. "The Cotton Candy Cowgirls!"

We made it.

TWENTY

Skarla, Barbee, and Micqui throw their pink hats in the air and catch them like prizes. Crazed screaming and applause erupts around me. People I don't even know rush over, hugging, congratulating, smothering. It's like I'm starring in a movie about someone else's life. Why is being hugged by strangers a good thing? It's overwhelming and I don't know what I'm feeling—except a strong urge to escape.

So I do.

Slinging my guitar over my shoulder, I go to find my mother. When I was onstage I scanned the audience for her, but with the blindingly bright lights in my eyes all I saw were faceless shadows. Making my way down the center aisle, I search the mob scene for Mom. I don't see her, but who I do see makes me stop.

And stare.

Why is Jay Blankenship coming out from backstage? No one is up there anymore.

He isn't wearing his letter jacket or his Reaper mask, just

black jeans and a blue button-down shirt. Clothes that don't draw any attention. My suspicion sharpens when he glances around as if he's guilty of something. He has no official connection to the contest, and his Jay-Clone pals left the stage before our group performed. So why was he there?

Before I can decide whether or not to follow him, someone grabs me from behind in a tight hug.

"We made it!" Ruby's long black hair flies around her face as she jumps up and down excitedly. "Isn't this like the best moment in your whole life?"

I hardly know what to say, but I manage a smile. In all the craziness, I didn't realize until now that her name was one of the ten announced. I'm genuinely happy for her—only I'm bummed, too, because when I turn back to look for Jay, he's vanished into the crowd.

Did he have a legitimate reason for being backstage, or was he trying to cause trouble for Philippe again?

"Thorn, you were amazing!" Ruby exclaims. "I'm so glad we both made finals."

"Way cool. You deserved to make it."

"I didn't think I would. I nearly fell over when my name was called."

"I wasn't surprised. Just be sure to pick the right song for finals."

"Oh, I will. I already have something special picked out," she says in a mysterious tone. She doesn't reveal what song and I don't blame her, since we're competitors.

"Good luck." I smile. "You're really talented."

"That's what we told her," a slim man standing behind

204

Ruby says proudly. He has a shaved head and a reddish-blond goatee. Beside him, a husky man wearing glasses nods enthusiastically.

"But you're prejudiced, and I love you both even more for it." Ruby gives them each a kiss. She introduces them to me as her two fathers, and I'm a little envious because she has two supportive fathers while I have minus one. But at least I have my mother, who finds me a few minutes later and gives me a congratulatory hug.

"You looked lovely and played your guitar like a professional," Mom says with tears in her eyes. "I'm so proud of you."

"Really?"

"I had no idea you could play that well without any lessons."

"Guitar's easy." I shrug. "Anyone can figure it out."

"You're wrong about that—it takes an ear for music. You're a natural, honey. Once your father gets a job—and he had an encouraging interview today—we'll check into lessons. I feel like a terrible mother, though, not giving you music lessons or buying you a modern guitar. That old thing isn't even electric."

"Don't knock my instrument," I tease, giving my guitar a fond pat. "I got this for a steal at a garage sale and it suits me fine. I just play for fun."

"You impressed the audience—especially me. How about we go out to celebrate? Feel like a triple-scoop ice cream sundae at Mel's?"

No one ever turns down Mel's ice cream, and I'm no exception.

But that's only the first celebration of the evening. Mom must have called home, because when I walk in the door the whole family is waiting with balloons. Our family bakers Amy and Meg present me with a strawberry cream cake with sliced strawberries spelling out *CONGRATS!*

My sisters have colored a large banner with pictures of a stick-figure girl (me) holding something that must be a guitar but looks more like a giant potato. Even Dad seems in a good mood and surprises me by slipping me a twenty dollar bill. I try to return it, but he won't take it back.

K.C. gives me the gift of a ride in his newly repainted Ranchero to Skarla's house, where the celebrating continues with music, dancing, and enough food to feed the entire state of Nevada.

I don't get to sleep until very late and wake up the next morning groggy. Stumbling out of bed, I reach for my zippered leather pants but then change my mind. I slip on a pleated sky-blue skirt and a white blouse my grandmother gave me for my sixteenth birthday, which I'd shoved to the back of my closet, planning never to wear.

At school, signs are posted all over announcing the big Singing Star competition on Friday evening, inviting the community at large to attend and displaying photos of the finalists. I stare at our Cotton Candy Cowgirls photo, captured during the audition. I barely recognize myself. The differences go deeper than just hair color and the cheesy western clothes. I am not there. Not the real me, anyway.

So why does everyone—including my own family—like this fake me better?

Rune isn't waiting at my locker. Guess she's still angry that I wouldn't tell her who the Grin Reaper is. She's totally not being fair. She should understand that this isn't easy for me. I need her support, not her sour attitude.

At lunch, I go directly to the cafeteria and sit with the CCCs.

With five thousand dollars and a shot at performing with Philippe at stake, rehearsing is critical. After school I catch a ride with Skarla to her house; she chatters excitedly about how great it will be to win and perform in Las Vegas. Nerves knot up like fists in my gut. I remind myself how much that money could help my family. So I play guitar until my fingertips feel raw. Our group sounds better than ever, and I have to admit (although not out loud) that the clogging is a good gimmick.

For being grounded, I've never spent less time at home.

By Thursday I'm exhausted, and my face aches from pretending to be interested when my bandmates talk about people I don't know, stores I don't shop, and TV shows I don't watch. Am I bored out of my brain by their conversation? You bet I am. I long for a heated debate about the lack of rights for migrant workers or how the government is using social networks to subliminally brainwash teens. I really, really miss Rune.

When best friends fight, no one wins.

So when the lunch bell rings, I ambush Rune outside her class.

"Hey, Rune," I say casually as I step in front of her.

She glares at me like I'm her worst enemy. "Get out of my way."

"No." I stand firm.

"What are you doing here, Thorn?"

"We're going to have lunch together."

"Sorry, but you have me confused with someone who doesn't hate you."

"Hate?" I snort. "That's harsh and really juvenile. Can't you do any better?"

"I could, but I'm refraining from swearing." She folds her arms across her chest. "Move aside now."

I don't budge an inch. "We have lots to discuss. Let's go to lunch."

"I'll tell you where to go!" she threatens.

"Where?" I arch a brow.

"To the cafeteria with your frilly pink friends. You deserve each other."

"Don't be a jealous bitch."

"Did you just call me jealous?" she exclaims, her hands on her hips in outrage. "I am not even a tiny bit jealous. What I am is disgusted. You keep secrets from me, and you traded in your soul for fluff-brains. I thought being goth meant more to you than a fashion choice—that you really cared about deeper things."

"If I didn't care, I wouldn't be here."

"So leave. I don't want to be seen with you—it's bad for my reputation."

"Afraid my new popularity might rub off on you?"

"You're not *that* popular."

"I hope so." Then I laugh, although I'm really not sure why. But then my laughter sparks Rune's. Her mouth twitches like she's fighting to hold on to her scowl, but then she's laughing, too.

"Okay," she says with a shrug. "I'll eat with you. But you can't make me talk."

"Fine. We'll eat our lunches in total silence. Don't say anything."

"I won't!"

We reach the stairs and sit on different steps. I dig my lunch out of my backpack and she flips open her vintage Addams Family lunch box. She peels an orange, the sweet scent swirling in a chilly breeze. I sip pomegranate-flavored water and glance at my watch, wondering how long Rune can go without talking.

Three minutes and seventeen seconds.

"You missed yesterday's *Weird News*." Rune opens her notebook of weird facts. "Want to hear it?"

"Sure. Bring on the weirdness," I say, smiling.

"A thirty-two-year-old woman breastfed her dog."

"Sick!" I almost spew pomegranate water. "That image has scarred my brain forever."

"Kids marrying dogs. People getting naked in strange places. Why do people do such gross stuff?" Rune gives a grim shake of her head. "The world is insane."

"Except for us," I say.

"Of course." We both nod solemnly, understanding each other.

I don't see her again until after school, when I find her waiting by my locker.

"You're coming with me and I won't take no for an answer," she says, tugging my arm once I've shut my locker. "I have someplace amazing to show you."

"I want to go but I have practice."

"It won't kill you to be late."

"Skarla might."

"Then I'll conjure a magical blood spell to bring you back to life."

"Okay, I'll go," I say. I'm sick of rehearsing anyway, and since my parents will think I'm with the CCCs, that whole grounding issue won't come up. "But keep the blood spell handy," I add. "I may need it later."

I borrow Rune's phone and tell Skarla I'll be late because of a test I have to make up (lying really is kinder than the truth). Then I climb into Rune's car and she zig-zags down narrow roads I've never been on before, parking in front of a ramshackle shop with a crooked sign that says simply, *JUNK*.

The store is a treasure trove! It's like someone opened a crypt of wicked-cool stuff and priced everything ridiculously low. Costumes, makeup, jewelry, and a giant skeleton of a grizzly bear that's freaking scary.

Rune and I "ooh" over a bin of wigs in every color and style imaginable. We try most of them on, modeling in our own twisted fashion show. A green wig transforms me into an alien, a long-black-braid wig wriggles like a snake against my legs, and when we try on skull caps we call it "bald chic."

"Let's go to school bald," Rune suggests as she taps her black-painted nails on her plastic-smooth head.

"We should paint fake blood dropping from our bald heads," I say.

"Check out these tombstone earrings." She hands them to me and digs into a box of old jewelry.

I nod. "Wicked brilliant."

Then Rune lets out a shriek. "Ohmygod, Thorn, you have to buy this!"

She's dangling a midnight blue wig, edged in black, in front of me. It's love at first look-in-the-mirror. The price isn't bad either (thanks Dad for the twenty!). Then Rune discovers a box of leather pants, tops, jackets, and even whips. We snap whips at each other until a store clerk gives us the evil eye, then we haul our purchases up to the counter. Rune buys tight leather pants, dragon earrings, and fishnet nylons, and I buy the blue-black wig, the tombstone earrings, and a Halloween zombie makeup kit. We both buy a whip.

Rune and I squeeze into a changing room and come out of the store wearing our purchases—we look very different than we did when we came in. When Rune tempts me with the offer of a donut at The Whole Truth, who can resist? Not me, that's for sure.

Over two double whipped-cream nut bars, Rune apologizes.

"It wasn't right for me to insist you break a promise," she says. "Although I'm dying to know who the Reaper is."

"I'll tell you when I can," I promise.

"Yeah. I know you will."

"I messed up, too," I add, licking cream off my upper lip. "I never should have ditched you. The CCCs are okay, but I can't really talk to them. Not like with you."

Rune takes a sip of iced tea. "Amerie is cool, but you're my kindred spirit. I'm so glad you moved here."

"I hated moving," I confess. "I still miss the color green, but I'm beginning to like cactus. And I never expected to find a best friend."

"It takes a rare soul to appreciate my coolness," she says with a pat of her skull cap. "It's like I can totally be myself with you."

"Yeah. Me too. Except lately I haven't felt like myself." I touch my eyebrow, smooth without its usual piercing. The CCC pink skirt rustles like a snake in the grass sneaking up to bite me.

Rune deserves the truth, I realize guiltily. I can't tell her about Jay, but I can share my own secrets. My three deepest secrets.

"Since I really trust you, I'll tell you three things about myself."

"Sure. What?" Rune's silver bangles clank as she leans across the table, her expression solemn.

"The first thing is my name," I confide. "It's not really Thorn."

"Well, duh, I guessed that. What's your real name?"

"My first name—don't you dare laugh—is Beth Ann."

She almost chokes on her donut. But she swallows fast and doesn't laugh.

I nod, relaxing a little. "Since I told you my real name, will you tell me yours?"

"Rune," she answers.

"No, really."

"Really honest-to-Goddess truth. The name on my birth certificate is Rune. My mother found it in a Wicca baby name book." She wipes her mouth with a napkin. "What's your second secret?"

"Music. I used to only sing and play my guitar in private." I shrug, then add, "But I guess it's not such a secret now."

"Not for anyone who saw you on stage. You were amazing."

"Thanks." I pause, knowing what is coming next and reconsidering this new honesty. How can I tell Rune about my finding? It's freaky and unexplainable. The only person who really understands what it's like to be psychic is Sabine.

What if Rune thinks I'm delusional?

"So what's number three?" Rune drums her black fingernails on the table.

I take a deep breath and spit it out.

"I'm a Finder."

"What's that?"

"A psychic ability."

"You mean you see ghosts?" she asks curiously.

"Not if I can avoid them." I shudder. My few experiences with ghosts creeped me out. "The technical term is psychometry. I get visions of how to find things when I touch objects. As a kid, I thought it was fun. I always won at hide-and-seek. Mom used to lose her keys a lot and I could always find them. Other kids babysat or mowed lawns, but I made money by finding lost pets, until a neighbor got suspicious and accused me of stealing her cat for the reward. That's when I learned to be cautious and hide what I could do. No one believed me, anyway." I meet Rune's gaze. "So the question is—what do you believe?"

"That everything is possible," she says. "I've never told anyone before, but I've seen ghosts twice. The first time was my great-aunt, who came to my room to read me my favorite picture book, *Two At The Zoo*, an hour after she died. Another time my cat Kiki, who got hit by a car, appeared on my bed and I could even hear her purrs. Does that happen a lot with pets?"

"I'm not an expert on ghosts, but it's cool you got to see your cat again."

"And your finding thing is cool. Can you show me how it works?"

"It's not a game." I glance down at donut crumbs on my plate. "Sometimes it leads to tragic things you wish you'd never found."

"Tragic?" She arches her pierced brow. "Like what?"

I shiver at the memory of a dirt-crusted blanket and tiny bones. "It's hard to talk about."

"No more secrets, okay? You can tell me anything."

"Well..." I bite my lip then give a slow nod.

And I tell Rune about the grave.

TWENTY-ONE

That sheriff is a moron if he suspects you!" Rune complains when I finish, the plate with her half-eaten donut pushed to the side.

"He said he doesn't, really. He knows I only moved here a few months ago. Still, he grilled me like I was a criminal."

"Why would he do that?"

"Because he wants to break me down so I'll tell him more." Uneasiness gnaws at my stomach. "He thinks I'm lying to protect a friend."

"What friend?"

I give her a meaningful look.

"You mean ... *me*?" Her kohl-shadowed eyes widen.

"I don't know, but it's no secret I hang out with you and Amerie. I didn't give him names."

"Still, if my parents hear the sheriff suspects me, I'm dead." Rune clicks her tongue stud with her teeth. "They're obsessed with their status in the community. I don't want them to lose trust in me or they'll take away my car, credit

215

card, and freedom." Rune grabs my hand. "Thorn, we have to find out who buried that baby."

"Duh." I roll my eyes. "What do you think I've been trying to do?"

"If the girl goes to this school, it shouldn't be hard to track her down. Do you have any suspects?"

"I had a lot, but now only one." I explain about the locket. "Skarla."

"Are you serious? But she doesn't even have a boyfriend."

"She did last year, but she acted secretive when the topic came up."

"A baby secret?" Rune touches her chin thoughtfully. "I remember hearing that Skarla had some kind of family issue last spring and missed a lot of school. This would explain why. Case solved. You should tell the sheriff that Skarla is guilty."

"Only she might not be. I don't have enough information."

"So use your finding radar to get proof. Aren't you meeting at her house tonight?"

"I should be there now," I say with a wry smile.

"I'll drive you over right now so you can spy."

"I don't spy," I say indignantly. "But I would love another look in her bedroom. If she took the locket, that's where it'll be hidden. Then I'll know for sure she's the one."

Rune jumps up. "I'll drive you."

We make it to Skarla's house in less than ten minutes.

When I reach up to take off my midnight blue wig and

jewelry, Rune stops my hand. "Don't change for them," she says. "I dare you to go inside just as you are."

"Not a good idea." I tap my dangling tombstone earrings so they swing like nooses against my neck. "The CCCs won't like it."

"Since when did that matter?"

"I don't know, it's just that lately … " I take a deep breath. "But you're right. It doesn't matter what they think about me."

"Or anyone else," Rune adds. "Be proud. Be gothtastic."

"That's not even a word."

"It should be."

Feeling more like myself, I wave good-bye to Rune, then follow the white gravel path to Skarla's door. There's a weird moment when Skarla's grandmother stares at me like I'm a stranger until her gaze falls on my guitar. Then she recovers with a quick smile and invites me in.

When I enter the family room, the CCCs stop clogging. The trio stares at me with expressions that could freeze sunshine.

"Look who finally showed up," Barbee says coolly.

"What happened to your hair?" Micqui frowns. "You were cute as a blond."

"I knew you'd revert back to goth freak," Barbee snarks.

"Barbee, shut up," Skarla snaps, then turns back to me. "Thorn, you aren't going to, um, look like that tomorrow. Are you?"

"Not for the show," I assure her.

"Okay. So we're okay." Skarla sighs with relief. "Now let's get to work."

We practice for over an hour before Skarla's grandmother announces dinner.

This is my chance, I think as I set down my guitar. But I need to play it cool so no one gets suspicious. I get a flash of the baby clothes in Skarla's trunk. I don't know if this is a finding intuition or my unconscious pushing me to do something. Could the locket be underneath the baby clothes or tucked inside a jewelry box?

Time to find out.

Using the bathroom excuse, since it worked before, I detour into Skarla's room and shut the door behind me.

There isn't much time. I visualize the golden locket, trying to trigger my finding sense. But I get nothing. I go around the room touching random objects: a lamp, shoes, a backpack, a jewelry box. Still nothing.

The baby clothes, I think. I need to touch them again. So I go to the trunk and lift the lid. I gently pick up a green knitted bonnet and hold it in my hands, closing my eyes and concentrating. A grave, a baby, something… I search my mind for answers.

Instead of a baby, I get a sense of a man. I squeeze my eyes shut, focusing on the soft clothes in my hands. A tall man with an anchor tattooed on his tanned forearm. He held these clothes… bought them. It's a fleeting thought, but one that feels right.

That familiar tingle of finding surges through me. Opening my eyes, I set down the clothes and let the urge lead me to a tall bureau near Skarla's closet. I empty my mind and my body moves on its own. I open a bottom drawer and rifle under heavy sweatshirts until my fingers touch something hard.

A photo album.

Flipping open the book, I stare at a photo of a man in sailor's cap and rough work clothes. His arm is around a slender woman who looks a lot like Skarla only she's older. I flip the page, but then stop when I hear a creaking door. I glance up just as Skarla screams, "THORN!"

I whirl around, all the blood rushing from my face.

"What the hell are you doing with my baby album?" Skarla demands. Micqui and Barbee stand behind her, glaring at me.

"Baby album?" I repeat, shocked that she'd admit this.

She snatches the book from my hands. "This is my private property. You have no right to be in my room!"

"I warned you about her," Barbee says. "But I didn't know she was a thief."

"I'm not a thief!"

"We caught you in the act," Barbee retorts. "What did you steal?"

"Nothing. I would never do that. I was trying to find something."

"What?" Skarla demands, in the coldest tone I've ever heard from her.

I purse my lips, trying to think of a believable answer.

"I thought you were my friend," Skarla rushes on. "I

invited you into the group and into my home. I deserve to know what's going on."

I stare at her, my heart aching because despite my suspicions, I like Skarla. But I need to know the truth, too. I gesture toward the trunk of tiny clothes. "I wanted to find out about the baby."

Skarla knits her brows. "What baby?"

"You already know. You hid the baby clothes and the album so no one would find out what you did."

"What the hell are you talking about?"

Skarla sounds so outraged I almost believe her act. But there's no other explanation for the hidden baby clothes. "You had a baby."

"A baby!" she exclaims.

"Don't deny it. I know the baby died because I found the grave."

Micqui and Barbee gasp.

"Ohmygod!" Skarla's hands fly to her cheeks. "You're the unidentified teen who found the baby's grave!"

"*Your* baby's grave," I correct her, then soften my voice. "I don't judge you. What you did wasn't easy. You must have been scared and panicked."

"*I was not pregnant!*" Skarla waves the photo album like she's going to hurl it at me. "That's the most ridiculous thing I've ever heard!"

"Then explain the baby clothes."

"I don't need to explain anything to you! But I will." She flips opens the album to the photo of the sailor. "This man is my father."

"Your father?" I whisper, stunned.

"It's the only picture I have of him. And those baby clothes were all he ever bought for me—before he left my mother and died from an overdose. My mother wanted to throw them out but my grandmother insisted on keeping them for me."

"You mean … you didn't have a baby?"

"Of course not!" Skarla's face reddens. "How could you even think such a thing?"

My mouth is open but I can't think of anything to say.

"If you suspected me, why not just ask?" Skarla demands. "Instead you lied and deceived me. I really liked you, Thorn. But this is unforgivable."

"Unforgivable," Micqui echoes, with a stomp of her foot.

"Told you so," Barbee adds smugly. "You can't trust girls like her."

"Leave, Thorn." Skarla points to the door. "You're no longer welcome in my house."

"What about rehearsal?"

"Rehearsal is over for you." She hugs the photo album to her chest. "Return the hat and costume tomorrow. You're out of the group."

TWENTY-TWO

I'd been dreading the finals, but now that it's over for me, I'm numb. I totally screwed up. I was wrong about Skarla like I was wrong about Ruby. I should leave the investigating to Sheriff Hart.

And I don't even have a ride home. My humiliation worsens when I have to ask to use the phone to call Mom.

She doesn't say anything until she pulls into our driveway and turns off the car. Then she turns to me and asks what happened. I thought I was hiding my emotions well, but her mom radar surpasses my sixth sense. And I cringe inside, knowing what I have to tell her. Mom was so proud of my being in the contest—the disappointment will cut deep. But by tomorrow night everyone will know anyway, when the Cotton Candy Cowgirls take the stage without me.

Staring at a ragged scratch on the corner of the leather seat, I tell her. I omit a few details, and just say that there was an argument and I got kicked out of the group.

"Oh, honey," is all she says, reaching over to squeeze my hand.

"Do you hate me?" I ask. Stupid tears spill from my cheeks. Damn.

"Of course not. You're talented and I'm proud of you."

"But I won't—" My throat tightens. "I won't be able to help with the money."

"What money?"

"If we won the $5,000, I was going to give my fourth to you and Dad."

Mom shakes her head. "No, you would not. Any money you earn goes to a college fund."

"But our family needs it and I want to help out."

"Your job is to go to school. If you want to help out, wash the dishes more often. Amy hates that job and I get sick of hearing her bitch."

"Mom! You swore!"

"So what? I'm a minister, not a saint."

"But you're always so ... so good. Not like me."

"You're not so bad," she says, with a playful tug on my blue wig.

"Then why did a stranger write letters complaining about me?"

"For your information, that busybody only used you as an excuse to stir up trouble. She hoped to get me fired so her husband could take the position."

"You *know* who wrote the letters!" I jump, bumping my elbow against the car door. "How did you find out?"

"Her husband brought her over to apologize. He

caught her writing another letter and was furious. We all had a long talk and I've promised not to reveal their names. But I want you to know that this was never about you. You were only a victim of church politics. I'm sorry you had to go through that."

"Sorry enough to unground me?" I ask.

Mom laughs, then says, "Maybe."

———————

The next morning, I fold the western fringed skirt and blouse into a box. I set the pink hat on top of the box. I'm still not sure if I'm more disappointed or more relieved about not being in the contest anymore. Maybe someday I'll play my guitar in offbeat pubs for small audiences. But for now, I have no aspirations for fame.

Pink is out. Black is back.

I zip into leather-studded pants, then drape a velvet black cape over a beaded blue top. Then I open the Halloween zombie makeup I bought yesterday and paint my face wicked shades of pasty white and bloody crimson. Slashes of dark blue eye shadow match my eyes and the midnight blue wig.

I survey myself in the mirror. Gothtastic.

K.C. and I leave for school early in order to drop off the CCC costume at Skarla's. When Skarla's grandmother answers the door, I shove the box and hat into her arms and hurry back to the car. The costume originally belonged to Priscilla anyway, and now she can wear it again. It never did fit right.

Lunch on the steps with Rune is the same yet different. She has her usual weird fact (a woman lost her toes due to frostbite and strung her toe bones into a necklace). But we have moments of silence, too. We're just comfortable hanging together and don't need to fill the space with words.

Then Amerie rushes up like a sudden wind storm, fluttering down to the middle step between us.

"I can't stay long," she says, her face shining as if she's glowing inside. "I have so much to get ready for tonight. But I wanted to see you both before ... well ... before everything changes."

"What's going to change?" Rune asks with sharp suspicion.

"If you're going to say something snarky about Philippe," Amerie threatens, "I'm leaving right now."

"Fine." Rune sighs. "He's perfect and I have nothing evil to say about him. Can we get past that now?"

"Of course! I can't stand it when we fight."

"You're the one who stopped talking to me," Rune reminds her.

"I know, and it felt awful. So much is going on and I want to share it with my best friends." She looks at me, her expression sobering. "Oh, poor Thorn. I heard what happened with the Cotton Candy Cowgirls. I'm so sorry."

"Don't be. I'm okay," I tell her.

"Don't pretend with me. You must be utterly devastated! How awful to be kicked out of your own group."

"It was never my group. And I'm *not* devastated."

"I tried talking sense to Skarla." Amerie rushes on as if

she didn't hear me. "I asked her to take you back, but she already has a replacement."

"Priscilla," I add. "Yeah, I know."

"It's so unfair! What did you do to piss Skarla off?"

"My tactful personality."

"How can you be so casual? If it were me, I'd be in tears. Your chance for fame and money is destroyed. You're so brave."

"Really, I'm not. I'd rather watch the show from the audience."

"So you'll be there?" Amerie asks hopefully. "I was afraid you wouldn't come. It's such a historic event and it would be tragic to miss it. Tonight is going to be life-altering amazing."

"But it's also the end for you and Philippe." Rune raises her brows as she studies Amerie. "When the contest ends, he'll leave."

"It's not the end for us. Tonight is going to be the best night of my life."

"What are you planning?" Rune asks suspiciously.

"I'll never tell," Amerie answers, in a way that's very telling. Then she jumps to her feet, her gauzy wings unfolding so they peek out over her shoulders, and rushes off.

Rune's gaze follows her until she flies around a corner and out of sight. "It's obvious what she's planning."

"I know," I say softly.

"She's going to be with Philippe tonight. Then, he'll leave tomorrow and she'll be destroyed."

"You can't stop her," I warn.

"I know, and it sucks."

The warning bell rings, and Rune balls up her lunch bag and tosses it toward the Dumpster. She misses and tries again.

"She'll survive." I shoot a high shot and my bag sails in.

Out of the corner of my eye, I notice a group of guys in blue letter jackets moving down a walkway. Even from this distance, I recognize Jay's confident stride. I think back to auditions and how he moved much more furtively, sneaking out from backstage.

And I think to myself, *Amerie's not the only one hiding secrets.*

————

The Singing Star contest finals begin at seven p.m.

Just enough time to go home, check email, and have dinner.

I delete spam, postpone reading the email from a goth friend back in Sheridan Valley, and click open an email from Manny. It's a photo of Skarla, looking svelte in a Lycra mini-dress last March. I groan. *Now* he sends me this? No wonder I didn't find the locket in Skarla's room.

The phone rings. It's usually one of Mom's parishioners calling for her, so I continue reading email until Mom comes into the family room holding out the phone.

"It's your friend," she says, then leaves.

Does Skarla want me back in the group? I think for a wild moment. Instead of being excited by the thought, I'm slammed with anxiety. My misgivings about losing my chance for fame are gone, now. Being kicked out was a good thing. I'm just not the diva type.

"Thorn, I can hear you breathing, so I know you're there."

"Sabine?" I smile. "How's everything?"

"I'm great, but what about you? I'm getting a weird vibe from you."

I switch the phone to my other ear and lean back in the chair. "Tell your psychic vibe to chill. Things have been crazy, but I'm okay."

"Good." There a rush of relief in her voice. "My spirit guide told me to warn you not to go anywhere tonight. I'm glad to find you at home and safe."

"No worries. The most dangerous thing I'm going to do tonight is watch a school singing contest."

There was a pause. "You're going out tonight?"

"Only to school."

"Don't go." She sounds so worried. I imagine her in her attic bedroom, holding the phone with one hand and twirling a curl of her long blond hair with the other.

"The only danger tonight is being bored by a few singers that stink." I chuckle. "Tell your spirit guide that I'll be fine."

"Seriously, Thorn, stay home. Opal saw danger from a gun."

"Get real, Sabine. We both know your spirit guide is all drama and doom. Why can't she predict good news?"

"She did have some good news for you," Sabine says defensively.

"What?"

"That you will 'soon achieve the highest success and ascertain a prosperous name in competition.'"

"Impossible. I was involved in one of the singing groups, but that's over now. There's absolutely no chance for me to 'achieve the highest success.' If she's wrong about that, then I'm safe from bullets. "

"I hope so," Sabine says. "But Opal's predictions have a weird way of coming true. So be careful."

"Aren't I always?" I'm chuckling as I hang up the phone.

As if anything dangerous could happen at a school singing contest.

TWENTY-THREE

In the auditorium, the crowd is insane. I'm no longer seated up front with the contestants but in the back, where a guy with linebacker shoulders blocks my view. I can only see if I lean into Amy, who's sitting on my right. K.C. is on my left, and he's straining his neck to get a good view too.

The seats are hard metal and press uncomfortably against the steel studs in my jeans pockets.

"Can't you sit still?" my sister asks when I bump her with my elbow.

"No."

"These seats are hard as rocks," K.C. puts in diplomatically.

"Harder." I cross my legs, then uncross them and stand up to stretch. Among the frenzy of people moving down the aisles, a familiar figure startles me.

I start to wave at Jay but stop myself. No one even knows we're sort of friends. But I lean sideways to watch him. He's wearing formal black slacks and a navy blue dress shirt and walking beside a distinguished-looking, salt-and-pepper-haired man who holds himself with the stiff bearing of a military officer. I don't need to be told this is Jay's father, the (not-so) Honorable Judge Blankenship.

"Who are you looking at?" K.C. asks.

"No one." I turn back to K.C., my cheeks warm.

"No one must be very interesting."

Very, I think as I swivel away from K.C. for another glimpse of Jay. But he and his father must have found seats. And why shouldn't they be here? The Jay-Clones are in the contest, so of course Jay would want to watch.

As long as that's Jay's *only* reason—and not to cause trouble for Philippe.

Lights flash across the auditorium, then flicker and dim as someone takes the stage. There's a hush, the audience eager for the star attraction. But it's only boring introductions. The principal, school board members, parent club president, and finally Collette, shimmering in red, take the podium. When she introduces herself and then Philippe, the audience explodes with fandom screams, whistles, and applause.

A spotlight shines golden on the star of the night. I smile, amused, thinking how only a few years ago he was just plain Phil, a troublemaker and dropout no one wanted around, but now people pay money just for a glimpse of him. Fame is like a mask, hiding realness beneath glamour. *Not for me*, I think, and I'm glad to be sitting in the audience. But stardom totally works for Philippe. He's dramatic and really hot in his tight jeans, and the black shirt under his leather vest has the top buttons unfastened. His white teeth flash as he takes the microphone to welcome the audience. Then he steps aside for Principal Niphai, who announces the first act.

Applause is muted for the first singer, Jaden Ming, then more enthusiastic for tiny, big-voiced Christiana Lee.

The Jay-Clones go on third, and as they take the stage the applause is so deafening I have to cover my ears with my hands. They did okay in auditions, but tonight their harmony is off and their clunky notes make for horrible chords. After a few minutes I want to cover my ears again, for different reasons. When they finish, the applause is only polite.

The next two acts are much better. Then the Cotton Candy Cowgirls are announced and I brace myself. My costume fits great on a taller, more full-figured girl with mocha skin and a big smile. Priscilla, the girl I replaced, has now replaced me. When I search myself for bitterness and find none, I realize with relief that I'm okay with this. Priscilla plays well … and loud. She rocks out on her electric guitar so passionately that I can barely hear the other girls sing.

The big dude in front of me shifts, blocking my view. The clogging is coming up and I don't want to miss it, so I lean into Amy. I still can't see the stage, but I have a clear view of the aisle—and out of the corner of my eye, I see Jay.

Why is he leaving in the middle of the CCCs performance? Where is he going? He's moving fast toward the exit … then gone.

Blast his conniving soul! He's going to cause trouble for Philippe.

I whisper to K.C. that I'm going to the bathroom, then I push my way down the row and exit the auditorium into the brisk autumn air. I look around the quad but don't see Jay. Clearing my mind, I focus my finding energy on him. Even though I usually need to hold an object, I can visualize him so clearly it's like I'm touching him with my mind

I move without thought, following a mysterious compass that knows more about my destination than I do. When I see a flash of movement turn a corner toward the parking lot, my inner alarm goes off. And I switch from a walk to a run.

In the minutes since Jay left the auditorium he's changed his clothes, switching into a dark cloak, black boots, and a concealing ski mask with a smiley face.

"Jay!" I call out.

He stops as if my voice is lightning and I've struck a direct hit. He whirls around. "Shhsh! Someone might hear you! What are you doing here?"

"I had a feeling," I say with a coy smile.

"Go back to the show," he tells me, punching a button on his keys the makes the lights flash on a white truck. "I don't have much time. My dad thinks I'm sitting with friends, but he'll look for me when the show is over. So I have to return before the last group finishes."

"Return from where?" I demand. "What's the Reaper plotting?"

"As if I'm going to tell you," he says, snorting.

"I already know your secret, so why not tell me more?"

"You'll tattle back to your winged girlfriend."

"I don't tattle to anyone."

"You'd warn her."

"Why are you so sure what I'd do?" I ask accusingly. "Is this about Philippe?"

"I should lie." He lifts his mask to look into my eyes. "But I won't. Not to you."

The sincerity in his tone softens my anger. And the way he's staring into my face shoots electricity through me. I see past the pretty features that mask the intelligent and volatile soul hidden deep within.

"What are you going to do to Philippe?" I ask.

"I'm not going to kill him, or cut off his famous curls."

I almost smile. "Then what?"

"Payback—that's all. Well deserved."

"Your opinion," I say, with heavy accusation.

"Don't try to stop me, Thorn. I don't want to do anything to make you hate me."

"Why not? You only care about revenge."

"You're wrong. I care about … ." He reaches out with his gloved hands and brushes a finger against my cheek; a touch as gentle as a feather, but it feels like sweet fire against my skin. "I care about more than you know. It's why I have to even the score."

I should move away from him, yet I don't. His gaze tugs and torments me with confusing emotions—curiosity, excitement, fear. As if he embodies the air at the edge of a cliff. What would it be like if I jumped?

Crazy thoughts, I tell myself. I'm only here because whatever Jay has planned for Philippe could hurt Amerie, too.

"Forget about revenge," I say quietly.

"Why should I?"

I shrug. "I don't know ... maybe because I'm asking you."

"That's a good reason."

"So you'll go back to the show?"

He gives a sad shake of his head and reaches for my hand. My fingers curl around his as if drawn to a magnet. An electric surge shivers through me and strange images whirl through my head: an image of us together, in a semi-dark room with striped red curtains and a fake-fur bear rug on the floor. We're not alone ... there's a sense of others in the room. And danger. The images flicker and fade away. But fear lingers, and so does a map in my head that's eerily similar to the map of where I found the grave.

Jay has been talking and I missed part of it. " ... Get something back, and this will be my only chance. I'm leaving now." He reaches up to pull his mask back on, and all I can see are those deep dark eyes. "Please don't follow me."

"I don't need to follow because I know where you're going."

"I seriously doubt that."

A puzzle piece clicks in my mind. "To 358 Red Hawk Drive."

His jaw drops open. "How do you know?"

"I'm psychic," I say as if joking. "And I predict you'll take me with you."

My prediction is one hundred percent right.

———

Since there's no talking Jay out of his stubborn revenge, I go along to make sure that whatever he has planned doesn't hurt Amerie. The drive is familiar, through dusky hills and shadowy trees and buildings. When I shiver, Jay turns up the car heater and offers me a spare jacket. I slip it around my shoulders, inhaling leather and Jay. I find myself looking at him in a new way. His full lips are pressed tight with determination as he stares out the windshield, gripping the steering wheel like it's an adversary.

When we reach the bend in the road where one direction goes up the canyon toward where I found the grave and the other winds into the half-finished housing development, I tense. Our headlights reveal a street sign for Red Hawk Drive, which winds through the skeletal houses and up the hill into the older area of homes. Some houses here have lights on. There are rock-and-cactus-decorated yards and parked cars.

A light green sedan is parked at number 358. Jay cuts his lights and rolls silently to the curb a few houses down.

"You stay here," he tells me.

"Like hell I will."

He shrugs and doesn't argue when I open my door. Moving stealthily close to the large decorative rocks, he creeps up to a window. Staying low, he peeks inside.

"What do you see?" I whisper.

He shifts to another window. "A light in the living room, but no one's there. The house looks deserted."

"What about the car?" I gesture behind me to the driveway.

"Must be an extra for when the family stays here. But Philippe and his crew have been staying in the bus and a hotel. No one lives here anymore."

"Philippe grew up here with his stepdad until he got a record deal and moved to L.A."

"Don't tell me you're a Philippe groupie?" he mocks.

I smack his shoulder. "Shut up. I heard it from Amerie."

"Damn. You got a powerful arm." Jay rubs his shoulder. "I'd ask you to wait while I go in, but I'd probably be wasting my breath."

"Totally. A big waste. I'm coming with you."

He nods, and I follow him as he winds around the backyard and goes up to a sliding glass door covered in dark beige drapes. He pulls tiny silver tools from his pocket, jiggles the lock, and silently slides the door open. We go inside.

It's not a large house—a modest living room opens into a small kitchen, and a narrow hallway leads to three doors. Jay pulls out a small flashlight and starts down the hall. He opens the first door: a closet-sized bathroom. He moves to the next door, shining the light into a very feminine room with a pale white carpet, a flowered comforter on the bed, a bright red suitcase propped open against the wall, and shelves overhead filled with hundreds of decorative porcelain plates.

"His mother's room," Jay murmurs.

"Before he moved her to LaLa Land," I add.

"One door left," he says.

We pause outside the final door and as my fingers brush the handle, I get a mental image of Philippe looking more like he appeared in the school yearbook; tough, with scars from fights and a mean scowl. Negative energy shivers through me.

The beam of Jay's flashlight lands on a wooden cabinet and he hurries into the room, which gives off a strong Philippe energy. *Philippe's old bedroom.* My footsteps soften as I step on a fake-fur bear rug. Drawers creak open and shut as Jay searches. Then there's a sharp intake of breath. I come up behind Jay as he shines his flashlight on stacks of vinyl records.

"Yes!" he exclaims as he pulls out a record. "We can go now."

"You only wanted a record?" I ask with surprise.

"It's a really good record."

"Valuable?"

"Not really—except to complete a vinyl collection."

"So why do you want it so badly?"

"To return it to Wiley."

"This is all because Philippe has an old record of Wiley's?"

"Phil borrowed it when he and Wiley were in a band together. Then Philippe found fame and took off for L.A. The singer on this record is Wiley's great-grandfather, and it's autographed to his mother. Wiley sent texts, wrote letters, and left phone messages, but big-shot Philippe couldn't be bothered to reply. So I left more direct letters and a DVD of Phil and Wiley jamming together. When they were in the band, Wiley helped Philippe write some of his songs, so I warned Philippe to return Wiley's property or the DVD goes on YouTube—which means everyone would find out that Philippe didn't write his bestselling song alone. Wiley doesn't even care about getting credit; he just wants his great-grand-father's record back. And now that I have it, Philippe can keep his secret."

"So let's get out of here," I say.

"Sure, let's—"

"Stop!" interrupts a shrill voice. "Don't move!"

The overhead light flashes on. I blink in the blinding brightness.

"I said don't move!" the woman warns. "Slowly turn around, both of you."

Her voice is familiar, and when I turn to face her I see red: glamorous red dress, ruby high heels, and furious crimson lips pressed tight. Philippe's manager, Collette, aims a gun at us.

———————

I remember Sabine's warning about a gun. Uncanny Opal was right again. Now it dawns on me that the red suitcase in the feminine bedroom was open. Collette must be staying here instead of a hotel.

"Put that down," Jay tells her, in a relaxed and friendly tone. He lifts one arm as if in surrender, but holds tight to the record with his other hand. "We're not thieves."

"Then why is your face covered? And what's with the smiley face cap?"

I move slightly in front of Jay. "I know this looks bad,

but you have to believe us—we know Philippe, and we aren't thieves."

Collette snorts. "Your masked friend has an album from Philippe's vinyl collection. Breaking, entering, and stealing! Yeah, that really sounds like you're friends."

"Philippe stole this record from Wiley Calderon," Jay declares. "If you check the autograph, you'll see it's autographed to Wiley's mother. Wiley's been after Philippe for two years trying to get it back, but his calls and letters were never answered."

"My client is too busy to bother with trivial manners." Collette waves her hand dismissively.

"Are you saying he never got Wiley's messages?" Jay demands.

"I protect him from obsessive fans, opportunists, and thieves." Collette barks out a sarcastic laugh. "I've already called the police."

"Good luck with that," Jay says wryly. "We don't have 'police' like in a big city, just the sheriff. And I saw him at the contest."

"We'll wait as long as it takes. You two aren't getting away."

"I only came here for the record. Philippe knows Wiley—they were in a band together," Jay says.

"Philippe used to run around with unsavory characters, just like you."

"He's telling the truth," I add. "I know Philippe, too. He's dating my friend."

Instead of supporting our case, this causes her face to darken. "If you mean that fairy freak Anne Marie—"

"Amerie," I correct, then match her glare. "And call me whatever you want, but do *not* ever insult Amerie."

"She's just another groupie who doesn't have a chance with Phil." Collette raises the gun higher and aims it directly at Jay. "Put the record down."

"This doesn't belong to him!" Jay repeats.

She smiles smugly. "We'll let the sheriff decide. Set the record on the dresser."

As Jay reluctantly reaches toward the four-drawer dresser, my gaze takes in several items scattered on top: a mirror, a brush, and some jewelry.

I stare in complete and astonished disbelief at one of the pieces of jewelry.

The golden locket.

TWENTY-FOUR

Oh my God!" I pick up the locket and dangle it at Collette. "It was you! You lost the locket on the stage, then stole it back. You have the nerve to accuse us of crimes when you're a thief and maybe even a murderer. *You* buried the baby."

All the color fades from Collette's face.

But she doesn't lower the gun.

"How do ... do you know about ... the baby?" she asks in a strained voice.

"I found its grave."

"*Her* grave," Collette corrects me, in a tone sad enough to break my heart—except that right now my heart is pounding like an army of drummers.

"The baby was a girl?" I ask solemnly.

Collette purses her lips, refusing to answer.

"Why bother lying?" Jay asks in a casual tone, as if there's friendship between them instead of a gun. "We're the ones who broke into your client's house and you can have us arrested if you want to. No one would believe us."

"Tell us what happened to the baby," I add, sensing that she wants to talk.

"It's none of your business."

"When I found it—her—" I swallow hard. "That made it my business. I need to know who she was and how it all happened."

A shudder seems to go through Colette, but she keeps a firm grip on her gun. "Okay, why not? We have time to kill."

I grimace at her words and glance over her shoulder at the half-opened door to the hallway. If we made a run for it, one of us could get away. Of course, the other one could get shot. Not great odds. So I try to keep her talking.

"Were you in love with Philippe?" I ask bluntly. "Was it his baby?"

"Don't be stupid," she replies coolly. "Only silly girls fall for his charm."

"But you must have loved him, because you had his baby."

"Ridiculous!" The gun shifts to me. "It wasn't me."

"Then who was it?" I ask.

"A groupie he met in Ohio. She threw herself at Philippe, then flipped out when he moved on to another girl."

"Rebecca?" I remember Manny's information about the broken-hearted girl.

"How do you know her name?" Collette asks, startled.

Jay chuckles. "Didn't you know? Thorn's psychic."

I cringe at his attempt at a joke but don't say anything.

I think hard, trying to understand the sequence of events. "Rebecca was pregnant? Not you?"

"Of course! Philippe has no common sense when it comes to his groupies. I warned him he'd better not put himself in this position again or he could find a new manager. Who else would cover up his indiscretions so cleverly? Philippe was relieved when I offered to handle Rebecca's accusations. He was going out with a famous model at the time and just wanted the rumors to go away. So I took care of Rebecca."

Collette grimaces as if remembering a deep pain. She's so lost in her thoughts that she lowers the gun. *This is our chance*, I think. The door swings open a little further, as if urging us to make a break for it.

But I hesitate, aching to know more. "What did you do to Rebecca and her baby?" I ask Collette.

"She wouldn't listen to reason, so I arranged for her to stay in this house with a midwife. We had an agreement that involved a substantial amount of money and an adoptive family."

"But something went wrong?" I prompt.

"Rebecca argued with the midwife and the idiot woman quit right before Rebecca went into labor—early. The baby didn't make it." A pained look crosses her face and she exhales deeply. "It took hours before I could catch a plane here, and when I arrived, Rebecca fought me when I tried to take the baby from her arms. I finally calmed her down with a sedative—then I dealt with the problem."

At least no one intentionally killed the baby, I think with relief.

"Why didn't you take her to a hospital or call 911?" I ask.

"And get hounded by paparazzi? Not an option. If we'd reported the death, the tabloids would have destroyed Philippe's reputation."

"So you buried the baby," I guess. "Then you threatened Rebecca or paid her off to keep quiet."

"I did what was necessary to protect my client."

"What about Philippe?" Jay interrupts, his black eyes narrow through his mask. "Didn't he care about his own baby?"

"He never cares about what he doesn't know," she snorts.

"You're wrong about that," says a cold, angry voice.

Philippe steps into the bedroom. Amerie trails behind him, her gauzy wings tilting as if broken. Her face is paper-white with shock, a sharp contrast to the mottled red fury of Philippe's. His lips press furiously tight as he strides over to his manager. "Collette, is what you said true? How could you not tell me?"

"Eavesdropping is beneath you, Philippe. Leave this minor problem to me."

"Just like I left Rebecca and her baby to you?"

I turn to see Jay's reaction—but he's no longer here. I catch a glimpse of shadowy movement beyond the door.

"You told me she was crazy and not really pregnant." Philippe glares at Collette.

"The result was the same," his manager snaps.

"No, it's not! I almost had a daughter I didn't even know about. If the baby had survived, would you have told me? I doubt it. You had no right to lie! And stop aiming that gun at Amerie's friend. Have you lost your mind?" He offers me an apologetic look and snatches the gun from Collette's hand, setting it aside. "I heard nothing about Rebecca for months, then I get a locket with a curl inside and a note from Rebecca that says, *Your daughter's hair*. My daughter!"

"The locket was yours?" I ask Philippe. "You lost it at school?"

"Yeah, but Collette found it for me."

I touch my neck where I'd worn the locket, knowing how Collette "found" it.

"I should have thrown the damned thing away when I had the chance." Collette gestures to the locket, which I'm still holding. I see the longing way Philippe is staring at it, so I reach out and hand it to him.

"Thanks," he says.

Beside him, Amerie whispers as if in shock.

"Your ... your daughter?"

"I didn't know what to think when Rebecca sent me the locket," Philippe says. "I figured it had to be her own hair—Collette had told me Rebecca was crazy and making up stories to try to get money out of me. I was going to trash the locket, but I couldn't ... and now I know why. Rebecca was telling the truth. Collette was the liar."

"I protected you," Collette says savagely. "When I told you I'd take care of your problem, you were happy to leave it to me. I always pick up after your mistakes. But I'm growing tired of your juvenile behavior. Don't think I don't know why you brought *her* to this house." She gestures to Amerie. "What lies did you tell her? The same ones you told Rebecca and countless other girls? That being together is the only way to prove your love? That you'll take her with you on tour? That you'll marry her?"

Amerie gives a sharp cry, as if she's been stuck.

I cross the room to stand protectively beside her. "Amerie, why did you come here with Philippe?" I ask gently.

"I … uh … we … " Amerie looks helplessly at Philippe. "When the contest ended, we left before he could be mobbed by fans. He said we could be alone … that he loved me … and I—I believed him." She steps toward him desperately. "Philippe … is it true?"

Philippe glances at Collette, then at the gold locket dangling from his fingers. Instead of putting his arm around Amerie, he moves away from her. "I'm sorry."

Amerie's eyes widen with shock and hurt, then disbelief. I hold tight to her hand, letting her know she's not alone.

"I've been stupid about a lot of things," Philippe tells his manager is an icy tone. "But it ends now."

"Are you firing me?" Collette asks with mocking amusement. "Because if you are, get used to handling your own problems." A smug smile curves her full red lips. "Do you hear that siren? It's the sheriff, finally showing up about a break-in. Would you like to explain what we're all doing here, and how this locket holds DNA matching the remains of a buried baby?"

Philippe's mouth opens, then closes. He steps closer to his manager.

"As I expected." Collette pats his arm the way a mother might comfort her child. Philippe may resent her lies, but not as much as he needs her support. *They understand each other*, I realize.

And finally Amerie understands, too.

"Thorn, I want to go home." She wipes away a tear. "Please."

I nod, slipping my arm around her fragile fairy wings. I guide her out of the room and look for Jay. I thought he'd be waiting somewhere. But when I look outside, his truck is gone.

Jay ditched me.

Collette does all the talking when Sheriff Hart shows up, and I'm in no position to argue. I brace myself for criminal accusations and am relieved when Collette apologizes for reporting a break-in. She says she didn't realize Amerie and I were friends of Philippe's. She doesn't mention anything about Jay.

To my shock, Collette brings up the topic of the baby's grave. I guess she would rather give her version of the story before anyone else can say anything. She tells Sheriff Hart she just heard about the baby's grave being found and can explain what really happened, but convinces him to wait until tomorrow and take her statement at his office. "It's been half a year already, so one more night won't hurt, right?" she asks, with a flirtatious charm that's more effective than a loaded weapon for getting what she wants.

Sheriff Hart agrees. They set up a time to meet and I suspect Collette will have a story all prepared for the meeting. The press will surely be there to hear her tragic version of the tale, in which instead of sounding like a lying manipulator, she'll come off as the heroine protecting her famous client from a disturbed fan. Philippe will be the tragic figure, who lost love and a baby he never got to see.

Justice will be served sideways—not all truth, but not all lies. And ironically, it works out for me.

But not for Amerie.

Philippe offers to drive us home, but I glare at him and shake my head. He's not getting near Amerie again if I can help it. I've noticed how kind and almost human Sheriff Hart is being to Amerie. He's not so friendly to me, but he's not hostile, either, which is an improvement. So I ask him for a ride home and he readily agrees. He helps me guide Amerie, who is sobbing, to his patrol car.

"May I borrow you phone, Sheriff Hart?" I ask in my most polite, minister's daughter tone. "My family will be worried."

"Of course," he says, unclipping a phone from his belt. "Here."

When the phone flashes on, I see a photo of a girl about my age with a black braid and gap in her toothy grin. Her dark skin contrasts with her very pale blue eyes. Immediately, I get a finding connection to her ... an image of a map showing central California by the ocean. And there's a girl kneeling on the beach—the same girl as in this photo.

"Your daughter," I hear myself saying to the sheriff, but part of me is still far away on a beach. "She's living by the ocean in a green trailer."

"What!" He jerks toward me like I've zapped him with a Taser gun. "What do you know about my daughter?"

My head is still in a fog and something compels me to say, "I know she misses you."

"What the hell!" He leads me over to the sidewalk, lowering his voice. "Who told you about Leannah?"

I consider lying, but have a strong feeling I need to be honest. "When I touch things, sometimes I get images about people and places. Weird, I know, so forget about it. I don't expect you to believe in psychic abilities."

"But I do believe," he says quietly. "I've worked with psychics a few times in my career. I wondered if you might be like that, too. Once I ruled out the logical scenarios for how you found the grave, it seemed like a possibility."

Now I'm the one who's shocked... and impressed.

"You really saw my Leannah by a beach?" he continues in a pained voice.

I nod. "You can call her and ask her yourself."

"No, I can't." He glances down at the photo on the phone. "She ran away from home four years ago. She never called or left any kind of message. I haven't heard anything from or about her... until now."

"I'm sorry."

"Don't be." He lifts his head. "For the first time in years, you've given me hope. And once all this drama"—he gestures back toward Philippe's house—"settles down, I'd like to ask you more about her."

"Sure," I say, then climb into the car beside Amerie.

It's not until I'm walking Amerie up to her house that I remember the Singing Star finals. "Amerie, who won the contest?"

"The contest? Oh, yeah." Her lashes flicker and a spark of her usual self returns. "Third place went to your group."

"My former group," I say with no regret.

"Priscilla played too loud, but they were still great. Although they would have done better with you."

"Thanks, but third is good. I'm glad for them."

"Second place went to the nerdy guy with the big voice."

"And first place?"

"Ruby Rodriquez." Amerie pauses on her doorstep and I'm relieved she's coming out of her zombie trance. "She sang this amazing song that blew the audience away. She said it was written by an unknown but very talented local song-writer. I can't get it out of my head. It goes like this."

Amerie sings words I've never heard before to a melody I know by heart.

It's *my* song. Only Ruby has added beautiful words to go with my music.

I think of Opal's prediction—that I'd "achieve the high-est success."

Not me, but my song.

And I smile.

TWENTY-FIVE

I sleep in the next morning and wake up to my little brothers playing Frisbee over my bed. And I know everything is back to normal—which is a good thing.

But it doesn't last long.

First Amerie calls, hyper-excited and not sounding heartbroken as she tells me to turn on the news. When I click on the TV, there's Collette's tragically sad face spilling her story, twisting the facts exactly as I expected. Philippe is destined to be even more famous after this scandal. When he starts to talk about his "tragic loss," I click off the TV. What a phoney-baloney jerk.

Then Rune sweeps in and drags me off for breakfast at The Hole Truth, because she wants the "whole truth." And I tell her as much as I can. Afterward, we go thrifting and I find some wicked black shoes with skull-shaped buckles for only seventy-five cents.

As I'm paying, I think about how even though I still miss my old friends from California, I've made some cool new friends here. My soul sister Rune is always amusing me with her wonderfully shocking weird facts, and Amerie is turning out to be made of sterner stuff than fairy wings. Nevada is starting to feel like ... well ... home.

On Monday morning, it's back to school. I wear my skull shoes and accessorize with skull hair clips and my black-blue wig. I put on blue lipstick and a temporary tattoo of a skull on my cheek. I leave the house feeling gothtastic.

Everyone at NB High is talking about Philippe and the contest, of course. Ruby isn't at school, and I hear she's gotten an entertainment manager and is planning her trip to Las Vegas. I find an envelope from her, though, in my locker. When I open it, there's a sheet of lyrics to *our* song with Ruby Rodriquez credited as lyricist and Thorn Matthews as songwriter.

Me. A songwriter. Cool.

As I'm reading the lyrics a second time, there's a tap on my shoulder.

I turn and find Jay.

I can't decide whether to slap his face or stomp away.

"Sorry, sorry, sorry," he says, blocking my way.

"You left me!" I accuse.

"Would you rather I'd waited around for someone to rip off my mask? Then the Grin Reaper would be done. I wouldn't be able to help people anymore."

"You didn't help me or Amerie."

"I would have, if you'd needed help. When I snuck out, I planned to come back and tackle Collette. But then Philippe took her gun away and I realized you weren't in danger. I hid outside until the sheriff arrived. If you'd needed me, I would have been there for you. Still, I'm really sorry."

"You should be … but I guess I understand why you left." I want to hold on to my anger, but finding out he didn't really leave means a lot. "Did you give the record to Wiley?"

Jay nods. "That big tough snake-tattooed dude cried when I placed it in his hands. He never thought he'd see it again."

"But you made it happen," I say, gazing into his face.

"I told you the Grin Reaper is a good guy." Jay clears his throat. "There's something else I want to tell you."

"What?" I ask softly.

"You aren't bound by your promise anymore. Now that everyone knows the truth about the grave, there's no reason for you to keep my secret."

"Oh, there's a reason," I say casually, like my heart isn't suddenly racing. "I kind of like having the Grin Reaper around."

"You do?" He gives me a slow smile.

"He's not such a bad dude when you get to know him."

"Want to know him even better?" Jay leans close so that our faces are inches apart. "If you can handle it, Goth Girl."

"I can handle anything or anyone, Reaper."

We look at each other for what seems like a long time, and I have a strong feeling that Jay and I are going to be something more than friends.

I'm not exactly sure what will happen.

But I can't wait to find out.

The End.

About the Author

Linda Joy Singleton lives in northern California. She has two grown children and a wonderfully supportive husband who loves to travel with her in search of unusual stories.

She is the author of more than thirty books, including the Seer series, the Dead Girl series, and the Strange Encounters series (all from Llewellyn/Flux). She is also the author of the Regeneration, My Sister the Ghost, and Cheer Squad series. Visit her online at www.LindaJoySingleton.com.

Also by Linda Joy Singleton